The Songs of Roland

The Return of the Cathar Magi

by

Richard Cirulli

CCB Publishing
British Columbia, Canada

The Songs of Roland: The Return of the Cathar Magi

Library and Archives Canada Cataloguing in Publication
Cirulli, Richard, 1952-, author
The songs of Roland : the return of the Cathar magi
/ by Richard Cirulli -- First edition.
Includes bibliographical references.
Issued in print and electronic formats.
ISBN 978-1-77143-357-0 (softcover).--ISBN 978-1-77143-358-7 (PDF)
Additional cataloguing data available from Library and Archives Canada

Note: All poems contained herein were written by Richard Cirulli.

Cover artwork credit: SelfPubBookCovers.com/Island

Publisher: CCB Publishing
             British Columbia, Canada
             www.ccbpublishing.com

To all true spiritual seekers of Divinities gnosis who walk life's arduous path with inner awareness, devotion, and a selfless veneration for truth and knowledge; those freethinking spiritual beings unshackled by the chains of ignorance, prejudice, convention, and the profane. The mystics society persecute with angry glee.

"If we believe we are giants among men...
why do we cast such short shadows before the gods?"
- Richard Cirulli

Contents

The Awakening

The past is a foreign country, a wasteland of nightmares and lost daydreams never found. The future is an unreality, since it has not arrived. It is within the present that our memories resurface from the deep and secret abyss of our soul. Here we contemplate, hidden from the scrutiny of our friends, about our past walks in this foreign land. A painful silent journey for honorable and honest men, who weigh the benefits of past affairs against the pain of sin. For me it was a self- and silent confession between God and me. I contemplated and questioned my existential life: will the heavens forgive me for my blind indiscretion and accept my sincere confession? Or will a vengeful God punish me for being a righteous man that once strayed? A just man is never ignorant of his sins, unlike the profane man who finds bliss in his sins, by rejoicing in his ignorance. Knowing sin and self-fortitude in the face of temptation makes a man just and wise. Denying sin, under the guise of ignorance, makes him just a man.

I found myself again in a fetal position as I tossed and turned in this sleepless night of another nightmare, my dark night of the soul. In confusion and self-doubt, this past memory passed through my soul and heart in conflict; for as the heart smiled upon this past pleasurable interlude, my soul was crying silently with cold tears.

She left me a voice message on my home phone last night. It has been a year since we said our farewells to each other – a rather mixed emotion, a zero-sum game – one must lose for the other to win, though winning came with many consequences and compromises. A shallow victory, at best a truce, as long as the secret was never revealed, even to the "winner," for emotional victories come without boundaries and definition. For in truth, it is only the lie that is the true victor, unknown to the aggressive and unrepentant "winner." A wise man knows that all that glitters is not gold. For you can place a gold ring in the nose of a fool and walk him through his heaven, and he will be unaware that he is standing in hell.

I pulled myself out of bed after another sleepless night of harrowing nightmares – a repeating dark dream and vision that visits me with increased frequency. I made no attempt to try to go back to sleep. It was 5 a.m. with a full Saturday schedule ahead of me. Looking for an escape of sorts, I walked over to my acoustic guitar and started strumming and picking at a blues song I was working on. I needed time to reflect, and make that decision I was hedging on. Should I return her call? Her voice was soft and friendly … as always … and sincere. I played it back a few times. She was a genuine soul with an equal heart at times too innocent. Her innocence and trust was betrayed by her naiveté. She was such a fond memory I wished to forget. Life never plays fair … and the stakes are high when emotions trump logic and restraint; this is especially true for sincere people who are honest with themselves who acknowledge the painful big step, the one that leaves a deep footprint on your soul.

I was not sure of her intentions. Was she in trouble? I had not really thought of her until last evening. I thought maybe the affair had never really ended and the winners were yet to be redeemed.

I have kept this affair to myself, guarded it jealously, never sharing it with my most intimate of friends and confidants. I am not known for my external emotions, refusing to wear them as a badge of weakness, or for self-pity to arouse the empathy of the well- intended weak. It is not my preference, or maybe I am just wired this way, always believing a silent heart with earnest actions trumps flippant emotions based on fragile egos.

My fingers tore up the frets of my guitar. I was unaware of what I was playing, mostly unconscious of my own presence. Maybe I was giving this far too much thought, why even the best of us fall to our passions when misled by circumstance. I always considered myself a moral person, God-fearing, though too humble to call myself a saint or martyr. I never viewed myself as a mortal sinner.

The hypocrisy of life is unfair. How does the honest man play the game of life fairly when he will be judged by the cheater and everyone else is cheating? The honest man will never find a fair consensus for his actions. The gentleman and moralist is not a superstar, just one who takes his guidance from restraint. Does not the gentleman share the same thoughts and fantasies as the womanizer when a woman of fancy passes his view? For if a gentleman would deny this, it would make him a liar and less of a man than the womanizer – for a womanizer never lies about his intentions, he always acts on them. Both share the same passions and temptations, and to a lesser degree the same objective, neither endorses celibacy, though the gentleman seeks love and fidelity.

Looking back, I am convinced not even a saint would have been able to resist her angelic looks. Her beauty was natural – blond hair, blue eyes, Nordic skin and chiseled face, complementing her hourglass figure and long, well-formed legs. She had that Midwestern innocence; in her late twenties she could pass as the homecoming queen. She was far too wholesome to be a temptress, her character was too moral with a fidelity she could never compromise. Her looks and natural swagger were in contradiction to her pure-hearted character.

I would be lying to myself to believe I was never caught up with her beauty and innocence. The thought of having her never crossed my mind; she was happily married, and always speaking well of her husband. Her natural innocence and good character always trumped her beauty. I never step on another man's turf, especially when deep emotions are at stake. I never play with a person's emotions! That is the golden rule I follow without compromise, and guard jealously. Just the thought of breaking this rule stirs my soul like a will-o'-the-wisp. If I coveted her, I was a sinner nonetheless. A guilty eye is not pardoned by restrained hands.

It was just one night of circumstance. Can one ever be right when correcting a known wrong? When one tries to do well, by attending to another's broken emotions. Was I her emotional savior? Or just a lustful demon masquerading as her guardian angel. What devil has made her his fool as well as me by proxy? We find ourselves at times as unknowing victims of sin, as we stumble over our fallen crown of sainthood. Her smiles were never a mask that could hide those hurtful tears of betrayal she could never hold back.

I am far too existential to accept life at face value, ever so self-critical and self- effacing. It is this self-assessed criticism that raises the bar of my character and integrity always outside the shallow bandwidth of mankind's unfathomable shallowness.

I am not one to feed off the emotions and vulnerabilities of others, regardless of my hunger. I am always over-thinking, contemplating my actions, and more importantly, the consequences for all involved. I am never egocentric in my actions. My own self- imposed act of contrition of sackcloth, ashes and self-flagellation, affords me no forgiveness –

regardless of my self-inflicted penance. My personal inquisition of my soul exceeds heaven's forgiveness.

My fingers ripped off blues licks faster than I could think thoughts of self-forgiveness. After all she forgave me. Who is the victim here? As I look back now, it was such a fond and innocent memory – am I not the better man for having made love to her? Even if just for a few days of bliss, she was my sanctuary in this cold and heartless world. Was she heaven sent? Or was I hell bent? Happiness is never static, its definition ever changing, and even compromised at times. Happiness is a dynamic emotion that can never be measured without sadness. Even honorable happiness at times comes with true guilt – even if just imagined. Did I take advantage of her true vulnerabilities? Or did she use me as well, to be her emotional pillow as she fell from paradise?

We were both victims of the moment – I even fell for the most common of lies– she believing I was her guardian angel pulling her soul out of hell. Or was I a fallen angel, naïve to my righteousness, tempted by her broken heart seeking the caress of salvation? Or were we just pawns of life's synchronicities, both sharing in a universal punishment? Is one to respond to a liar with truth? Or give fidelity to a known adulterer? For the sake of justice, there are times when the lines between right and wrong are grey – even contradictory. When do two wrongs make a right? Who is the better man, the one who stands up against aggressions, or the one who makes peace with transgressors in plain sight of the shattered victims?

My blues licks became more melancholy, with more tension applied to each note I fingered. To some degree it was my confessional song, unable to pardon my restless soul.

My thoughts began to flame like burning charcoal, intermittent and feverish. I thought, how is she doing? Is she really happy? I would only know if, and when, I returned her late-night call.

I finally composed my thoughts, and made the decision to face another day of trials and tribulations. I showered and dressed. It was a beautiful autumn day, sunny, cool, the foliage in full bloom. I then remembered it was almost to the day when I last saw her and held her in my arms, as I contemplated whether to let her go. I believed I would never hear from her again, least of all have her reach out to me for a rendezvous. She had never called to reclaim some of her intimate wear she left behind. I never kept them for any sentimental reasons or as souvenirs, or trophies – they were left there like most items in a junk drawer.

By the time I headed out for my boring Saturday morning errands I still had not returned her call, or for that matter Nancy's, inquiring as to what time I was picking her up tonight for the B.B. King concert at the Bardavon Theater. We were celebrating our second month anniversary – I was not chomping at the bit. I was pretty certain this relationship would be short lived. I always get this bad vibe from her when we are out in public. She always seems to be hiding a rather mysterious past – I could just sense it. She was not placing her cards on the table as we agreed going into this relationship. I was confused and in self-exile of my emotions. I had two women awaiting my return call, neither of whom I really wished to speak with.

In my reverie of self-contemplation, I went for a ride with no intended destination. The errands could wait for another day. I was pretty much oblivious to where I was; I just drove to clear my mind, trying to outrun my conscience that was always in my rear view mirror. By force of habit I tuned into my favorite blues station to pull me from my escape. I caught the beginning of a John Lee Hooker classic, *Boom Boom Boom*, and turned up the volume in hopes of drowning out my thoughts.

I found myself singing along to the song that pushed me down my slippery slope. It was so Zen, or synchronicity gone astray. Confused by all the cross-talk going on in my head, I made an unlikely stop at an old haunt. I pulled in the parking lot and approached the massive medieval Romanesque doors, not sure of my intentions and what I was hoping to achieve, or what I was trying to gain.

Confessions

In the silence of a doubt
I came upon a thought

That challenged me about

A thought of a sensual dream
As profound as sin
It stirred my soul
Once serene within

Like a night bird's fluttering wings
Seeking the nectar of the night
My fledging feeling
Now held me tight

Like a rose that blooms
In the maturity of one's life
Within my soul's conscience
My thoughts of rapture
Stumbled upon the thorns
Of my lost righteousness

My soul, once like clear waters
Of a calm glistening pond
Now ripples with past thoughts
Of rapture to respond

Roland

"Bless me Father for I have sinned, it's been a very long time since my last confession."

"Has it been that long? How long?"

"Yes Father, rather long."

"Are we talking years?"

"No disrespect, Father, it has been a few decades or so."

"I see, why the change in heart?"

"Well. Father, to be honest, does one need to be a Catholic to offer a confession?"

"Well, sir, you try my patience. Are you mocking me and my faith? As a lapsed Catholic, I am sure you remember it's one of the sacraments of the Mother Church?"

"Father, no disrespect intended for my pilgrim Church. I was raised Catholic, attended Catholic universities. I even worked my way up to professor and department chair of a Catholic university. I also raised my two daughters in the Catholic faith."

"Well, sir, the Mother Church seems to have prepared you well in life. You are blessed and successful. Please tell me, have you lost your faith?"

"No, Father, I believe I am a good Christian with virtues and good morals, too humble to believe I am righteous and free from temptations."

"Uhummh, before I take this any further, I will need to ask you a few questions. You appear earnest in your quest for penance. You say you are a good Christian. What brand of Christianity do you profess – if any at all?"

"Well, Father, I am a Mormon."

"My dear sir! You are no Christian at all. Why, your biggest sin is apostasy! Your sin is against God and the true Church. You are nothing but a fool following a cult figure and false prophet. I cannot hear the confession of an apostate who does not believe in the Holy Trinity, but believes in many gods, even believing men can become gods! Obviously you have learned nothing from our hollowed Catholic institutions.

Why don't you run to your imposter bishops for forgiveness? You must have committed quite a sin to return to your true faith – what sins do you wish for me to hear and absolve you of? Besides being a heretic? So tell me Mr. Good Gnostic Mormon, what do you consider as sins? I am sure it pales from that of following that fool and whoremaster Joseph Smith. So now that you sparked my curiosity, pray tell why this unscheduled stop and feeling of remorse. Are you in some kind of big trouble with the law? Did you kill someone? So why are you here?"

"Well, Father, I am guilty of coveting my neighbor's wife."

"Did you just lust for her, or did you have an affair?"

"Guilty on both counts, Father."

"My dear sir, do you feel any genuine remorse?"

"Yes, Father, deeply. It is a sin I thought I would never commit. Father, is it a sin if one sins not knowing it's a sin?"

"My dear sir, no good Christian can ever be ignorant of sin – not even a fool. If I were you I would take it up with a bishop of your heathen church. With a church that supports plural marriages, you may find yourself a hero. Just tell them the married woman you had an affair with was your spiritual wife – why, heavens, they may even make you the next prophet."

"Father, spare me the criticisms and your self-righteous sarcasms."

"Sorry, I see your confession is earnest. You admit to having an affair with a married woman. Was it planned? Premeditated? What was your intention and circumstance when you found yourself with her?"

"I actually believed I was helping her with her emotional trauma."

"My dear sir, how did you meet her, get involved with her in the first place?"

"She was a student of mine."

"Ummh did this take place at your Catholic university?"

"Yes father."

"Did you overstep your bounds of authority, to inflate her grades for sexual favors?"

"No, Father, it occurred after the grades were submitted."

"Were you at any point able to prevent this reckless and selfish act?"

"Yes, Father."

"Did you make any effort to try?"

"No, Father."

"Are you a married man?"

"Divorced, Father."

"Did you ever cheat on your wife?"

"No, Father."

"Have you cheated on any of your girlfriends?"

"No, Father."

"Was this woman much younger than you?"

"Yes, Father, by twenty-five years."

"Were you caught up in her beauty, trying to relive your lost youth, a mid-life crisis possibly?"

"No, Father, I am a realist, and chase not younger women in folly. I fell for her soul and the emotional pain she was going through."

"Is she a Christian of good standing?"

"Yes, Father – better than I – a good girl Idaho born and raised in a strict Methodist family. Father, I cannot deny or hide my actions, I am a disciplined man, and know better. Is sin defined not by the act but rather by place and time? Does not the God-fearing man pick up the sword to fight the devil for a holy cause? Or does our killing the devil makes us his possession?"

"Sir, how long have you been divorced? Are you experiencing the pain of its aftermath?"

"No, Father, I am quite happily divorced. My marriage was not heaven sent. I endured it longer than a fool."

"Sir, you sound like a wise and earnest man with a genuine God-fearing soul, burdened only with the sins of your own harsh self-judgments. Is not the pain you bear sufficient penance for your actions? Your misguided sin was well intended and selfless, though brought on by love for another human being in distress. Is not love the mark of a good Christian?"

"True, Father, your words are encouraging and kind. I am a man of high expectations and restraint; though I agree with you without reservation. But what is greater than this love? Only the pain of self-hate it bears on my soul. Father, confession may remove the guilt but never the sin, and the dark eternal stain it leaves on the soul."

"My dear man, what cross have you chosen to bear, one of penance or self-righteousness? You tell me you are happily divorced, though you choose to wear a mask of sorrows. Your morality is enviable; don't you Mormons read the New Testament? Do you remember the parable of the prostitute who was caught and was ready to be stoned? Do you remember

Christ's rebuke? 'Let him who is without sin cast the first stone.' Why do you cast stones upon yourself, just so you can overindulge your penance? Who applauds or respects a martyr who executes himself for self-glory – not God's glory? If we were all saints we would not need God. Why do you persist with wearing your sackcloth and ashes, while you wrestle about the ignorance of sin?

Let me leave you with a Buddhist saying I learned while in Nepal: 'It is more serious to sin unintentionally than to sin knowingly.' But let me also leave you with a Catholic saying: 'It is not the seriousness of the sin but the sincerity of the confession that is one's penance.' What is more unforgiving is the belief one can never sin. I bless you, and hope you make peace with your love conundrum."

I easily found a place to sit in the empty church, just to contemplate my next action. Will we fall into another adulterous affair if I elect to return her call and meet with her as she requested? Her voice message said it was urgent, that she had some important news she needed to share with me. Maybe she just wants to tell me she was accepted into graduate school, or she's having a baby. Heaven knows, maybe to inform me she confessed our affair to her husband. In my stream of consciousness I was lost in my own indecision. I left the church feeling more at ease having my confession heard, though not feeling absolved of my sin. I was still uneasy as to how I should handle this call. I was not sure what was getting the best of me, my curiosity of what she had to say, or the reservations and consternation of getting involved in another adulterous affair.

"Tested and tried is the path of cheating by means of a friendship,
though tested and tried, nevertheless, it's a sin;
proxies can go too far, being more than innocent agents."
- Ovid

On my way back to my loft, I went to an isolated grove overlooking the Hudson River, a place I frequent for meditation. I felt confused, guilty, and pondered in my soul whether my ever-increasing nightmares were my punishment for my indiscretion. I stood on the shallow bluff on the riverbank, faced east, got on my knees, took out my Cabalistic Talisman scribed on parchment paper, and began my invocation.

Isle of Elohim

The distant shore to be sought
The eternal paradise of the righteous man's journey
The most holy garden set upon the ordained sea of truth
Whose sweet fruits of virtue nourish my hungry soul

Holy Havona, majestic mountain abode of the most high Adonai
Isle of the most glorious son
Whose heavenly brilliance beacons the multitudes of the blessed
And where, the tranquil waters reflect
the consciousness of the Almighty

Hallowed isle with your never ebbing tides of unconsciousness
Absorbed by the alabaster sands of never ending time
Whose ivory columns of strength, beauty, and wisdom
Eternally support your most holy name

Shaddai el Chai, unite my spirit with your immaculate shores
May I be worthy to drink the sweet waters
of your overflowing font of ecstasy
May I be blessed to travel upon the valley of the ancient spirits
To hear the haunting winds that sing your glorious psalms of peace

Most holy Gabriel I call upon thee to invoke the heavenly winds
To fill my sail, to guide my vessel to the
sanctuary of your most sacred harbor
Metatron carry my soul to the most high mountain of Kether
To meditate on the most Holy Tree of Life
Rooted in the consciousness of Eheieh
Whose branches bear your heavenly harvest
And, evergreen leaves that offer shade to my seeking soul

Your Holy mount with its snow-capped mountains
With heaven's Holy waters eternally fills
the warm springs of the spiritual Zion
May my prayers and burnt offerings be
worthy to ascend your Holy Mountain

Ashes to ashes … dust to dust
Upon thy Holy hill I commend by soul to thee

For the Mahl-koot,
Vih-G Boo-Rah, and
Vih-G Doo-Lah are yours almighty God
Lih-oh-lahm

Amen

Nancy's text pulled me from my meditation, asking me to call her right away. I'd never returned her call from last night, either. She thinks I must be ignoring her calls, since I always returned them ASAP in the past. It is really unlike me not to return her calls – especially on a Friday night. She has been pushing for a more committed relationship, wanting to move in with me, or to stay over a few days during the week, which I have been reluctant to commit to. I told her I am not ready for her to move in at this time in my life. She thinks I am not serious about the relationship – she is right – and getting a little edgy, she is looking for a real commitment. Too be honest, I do not have a good feeling about her. I do not get the feeling she has placed her cards on the table as we agreed at the onset of our relationship. She is hiding something and I would prefer to expose it before the relationship goes any farther. After a disastrous marriage I was not looking forward to another bad relationship. I am seriously considering ending it before it is too late, and to get out without the drama and hard feelings. Besides we are very different people and she is ten years my junior. At this time in our lives neither of us are ready for a real relationship, though she is in denial.

I returned Nancy's calls when I arrived at my loft.

"Hey, Nancy, it's Roland. Sorry I did not get back to you sooner."

"So, Roland, where were you last night. Too busy to call me on a Friday night? You know I had the kids, you could have at least called to see how I was doing. Besides, where the hell were you last night? Hanging out with your artist friends – euphemism for lady friends – at Demitasse Café?"

This was the first time I experienced her suspicious nature and inquiring haranguing.

"I didn't arrive home till late from having dinner with some old friends in the city I have not seen in while."

"Well you still could have called me or texted me you know; it's not like you not to call. Everything all right Roland? You sound a bit down. Where are you now?"

"No, Nancy, I am fine – just a bit overworked and tired, have a lot of errands to take care of. Don't have much time to talk. I made reservations at the Rhinebeck Inn for this evening for after the show. I want to make it a special night Nancy. A day we can long remember. I will pick you up at your place at 6-ish. Be ready. I don't want to be late for the show."

"I'm excited, Roland. Now who are we seeing again at the Bardavon?"

"B.B. King"

"Who is he again; I'm really not into the blues, whatever that is. More of a Beach Boys kind of girl."

"I am sure we will have a lot of fun, Nancy, regardless of the music. Don't forget to pick up something sexy to wear for this evening, I like surprises."

"So Roland, does this tantra ummh *Kama Sutra* stuff have a proper dress code? Uummhh … honey?"

"No Nancy, just your flesh and warm probing hands."

"Hell, you know, Roland, I am not sure if you are a natural romantic, or just a horny old man."

"Well, Nancy, a little of both. It's not such a bad combination; it's in my gene pool. Besides 52 is not actually old … you know."

"Roland you're 53. You're the math guy, can't you professors count?"

"Quite well, Nancy, I am counting on you to satisfy my never-ending lust."

"Now, Roland, have I ever disappointed you yet? Tonight I will be you your temptress and lover. Well, professor, I can't wait for your next lesson ummmh – will you be able to restrain my passions?"

"Well I am sure it will be a very special evening for both of us, Nancy, one to look back on for years to come – got to run – see you later Nancy, and please be ready on time."

"O, Roland before I forget to ask, how about if stay over at your place till Monday evening. We can spend more time together, and I could find a place for my personal belongings. No need for me to always take an overnight bag. This way I can just drop over and get to spend more time together."

"Nancy, we went through this already. It is too early in the relationship; I am not ready for this type of commitment at this time. You know I am never home, and the few times I am, I have my friends drop over or entertain guests. It will not work at this time."

"O, Roland, well since you are away a lot, I can have my friends come over and visit me to keep me company. And besides, it's a nice place for my kids to crash."

"Nancy, this will not work, it's an artist's loft, I have my office here, my gallery for my artwork. This is not a home it's a museum, library, and my sanctuary. Not very practical for domestic arrangements. I have a lot of valuables here. Nancy, we went through this before."

"Well how long do I have to fuck you, Roland, to make it work?"

"Nancy, there are not enough days in eternity to give you this option. I will come over when I am through with my errands and paperwork."

"Roland, give me some time, I need some time so I can plan my day. I have a lot of errands, so I don't want to rush back for you, got things to do."

"Well do what you have to do and I will let myself in through the back door?"

"Roland, please, not before 6:30, OK – promise me OK."

"Hey why the formality all of a sudden, Nancy?"

"Roland, 6:30 not a minute sooner – promise?"

I hung up the phone, with a strong inner desire to call her back and cancel our "special" evening. Nancy's behavior patterns were sounding all too familiar – throwing up another red flag daily.

Nancy is too much of a materialist for my taste, shallow, small radius of knowledge and interests. Not the least bit spiritual or existential, not sure if she even holds a degree, though she claims to. I never pushed it, what little knowledge she has is well defined by her conversations. Spends her days shopping, and living off generous alimony and child support from her ex-husband. She has few kind words for him, though I know he is a successful professional in the area. She never explained the reasons for the divorce – just that it was his entire fault. The more I thought of her, and looked back on her actions I knew it was time to move on, before I get drawn into her life of drama.

I spent the day doing the typical dreaded Saturday morning bachelor errands – well at least the essential ones – the others can wait till next weekend, I am sure I will have more time then? I should just hire a maid.

In the afternoon I took my youngest daughter, Kymar, out for lunch to her favorite Korean restaurant. She wanted to talk to me about a certain problem she is facing at work. I was happy to see her, though she was astute enough to see the confusion on my face. She did inherit my family's intuitive, psychic gene. She cut the lunch short, saying, "Hey Dad, let's connect at another time.

Looks like your problem is a bit more pressing than mine. Will call you during the week? It can wait."

"Give my best to your mother."

"Dad, do you really want me to call you with her response? She is off her meds again."

Driving home I was still vacillating over whether to return the call. The last time I saw her, I believed would be our last. I was confident she would never want to reach out to me again. Why the change of heart? The urgency, what does she have to tell me? What have I got to gain? What have I got to lose? How destructive or difficult can a simple call be, after all her first calls were transforming – as sin. Though the more I thought of her the more I recalled those beautiful moments, our innocence – so we believed – and erotic times together. More of a reason to call her back, more of a reason to sin. My mind drifted to a nice place, I could not stop thinking of her. I began to softly think of that song that brought everything in focus for me ... even the sin.

THE CALL

I looked out of the third-floor window of my artist's loft that offered me a majestic view of the Hudson River and the foliage. I was trying to compose my thoughts before I made the call, or maybe it was just an unconscious delaying tactic. My thoughts drifted between my former lover and Nancy. Both were a conundrum of shorts, the former were of fond memories despite the fact she was married, The latter, an attractive woman in her forties who I am having ambivalent feelings about, and do not have any great feelings for. She is not an empathetic person, or caring. She is attractive and comfortable with her sexuality. I still have an uneasy feeling about her, or maybe I am becoming more critical in my old age? It seems like I have many options – though few choices.

She had also sent me an e-mail flagged 'Confirm receipt.' I opened it without hesitation.

Roland, please call me it's important I will only be in town for a week or so. We need to talk ... to set the record straight – we need closure. Dam you Roland call me! More for your sake than mine.

I replied,

Sure when do you want to talk?

I picked up the phone on the first ring.
"Well, glad to finally hear your voice, Roland. I was starting

to doubt you were ever going to take my call. Is everything alright?"

"I am doing just fine; it is nice to hear your soothing voice again. How are things on the home front?"

"Hey, Roland, you still can't be upset with me? Can you? It has been a year now. I thought by now you would have gotten over that guilt thing. Have you, Roland?"

"Well to be honest, I still have not forgiven myself."

"So, Roland, you are still playing the martyr, while throwing stones at me to make yourself feel better?"

"So share some of your good news with me!"

"Well, Roland, I will save the real good stuff for when we meet for dinner, my treat."

"Well, first of all, I should thank you for helping me get into graduate school; I just completed my MBA thanks to you! Even took a few electives in social economics ... aced it, thanks to you. Hey, Roland, if it makes you feel any better, those Ivy League professors have nothing on you, so try smiling and stop being so self-effacing. They never challenged me the way you can, Roland. So I am not taking no for an answer. When are you free this week?

O heavens, Roland, I forgot to ask are you married, or have a woman houseguest in earshot?"

"Why would that matter, it has not stopped us before?"

"Now, Roland, just knock it off, I called you because you mean so much to me, more than you will know. I just want to thank you personally, and share some really interesting news with you. Believe me; you need to hear this, more for your sake than mine."

"I am sorry, don't mean to be defensive; rather tough day. Yes, I would love to meet you for dinner. What is your dinner plan?"

"Well, Roland, just for old times' sake, and to rekindle old memories and feelings ... ummh, how about the place where we said our good-byes.

"Demitasse, how can I forget?"

"What does your schedule look like over the next week, Roland?"

"This weekend is a little tight; will you still be in town next weekend?"

"I will not be heading back to Idaho till next Tuesday, Roland."

"Synchronicity at work, I would say."

"OK, Roland, next Saturday, 7:30 p.m., Demitasse. Will reserve our favorite table by the window overlooking the Hudson – simply breathtaking. Besides, my second-most-favorite blues guitarist is booked there as well. Hey, Roland, I forgot to ask, you still playing out at clubs? I do miss your guitar work and sexy blues voice. Maybe you can play a song for me, just like you did at our first date ... was a John Lee Hooker tune, I believe?"

"Great memory, I can see why you had no trouble walking through graduate school. Yes, I remember that song well; it's the one that started this whole affair. Well, to be honest, I developed a bit of an indifference to the stage."

"Roland, you with stage fright? Now who are you kidding?"

"Aahhh, maybe just old age. O you did ask if I was seeing someone."

"So are you? Who is the lucky lady – Roland, will this create a problem for you?"

"No problem, she will not get in the way."

"Ummmhh, Roland, whatever happened, did you lose your Mr. Christian persona along with your desire to play out. Why, hell, Roland, that's how you get the women – well it worked on me, guitar/artist/ existentialist types. Sometimes I just can't figure you out, Roland. I could never understand how your existential and mathematical mind works.

So what's her name, Roland?"

"Nancy and I have tickets for the B.B. King concert at the Bardavon, then heading to the Rhinebeck Hotel for a romantic evening to celebrate our second month's anniversary."

"Sounds like a real serious relationship. Wow, Roland, you are in the longest relationship since your divorce, and you are losing your moralist persona. What's going on, I don't want to hear it's an aging thing, Roland. Do you love her?"

"To be honest, I really do not feel comfortable with her, something is amiss, just does not feel right."

"Well, Roland, what do you think it is? Is she sexy and amorous?

"Well to tell you the truth, aside from her looks and sexuality, we share nothing in common. I am having serious thoughts of breaking off the relationship. All I can say is I just get this uneasy feeling when I am with her, like she is not being forthright. She is very guarded with her past, very secretive, and very vague. She does not want to discuss it. I am not looking for details; just feel some big pieces are missing from her puzzle. I am not even sure what she does for a living. She will disappear for days, and not return calls. Has no interest in the arts, culture or intellectual discussions. I have never been introduced to her friends."

"Well it does appear odd on the surface, maybe you should give it a bit more time, or have a matter-of-fact sit-down – this is has always been your relationship MO; what is different here, Roland?"

"She is very evasive, changes the subject, walks away, or complains I am prying when I press her. She is spontaneous and fun – aren't all party girls? Aside from good, fun times, we have nothing in common. It would be a repeat of my marriage. And, we know in a serious long-term relationship, especially in middle age and maturity, sex becomes a smaller part of the equation each passing year."

"Well, Roland, you are a very intelligent, perceptive, and intuitive person. I believe you already made your decision."

"I am just waiting for the right moment to execute it in the more respectful way, free of the drama. Well I am looking forward to seeing you next Saturday, Candice, I'll pick you up at the airport. Feel free to call me if you need anything. By the way, what has your husband been doing with his life?"

"Will fill you in next Saturday, Roland."

The Barstool Blues?

As I pulled into her driveway, I noticed a plumber's van pulling out from in front of the house. It had some tacky logo and equally tacky phrase painted on its side. The Village Plumber … 24-hour service, flush with experience. As I entered the back door, I noticed the house was quiet, and her children were not at home. I heard Nancy in the bedroom, rummaging through her drawers, and trying to put her room in order. I also noticed a few empty vodka bottles on the kitchen table.

"Hi, Nancy, it's me. Are you ready, would hate to be late."

"O, Roland, I was not expecting you for a while. Caught me completely off guard. Why the rush, hell we don't have to be there for some third-rate opening act," she shouted from her room.

"I am just putting on my make-up, coming right out."

Before she could leave her room I went in to greet her, and give her a kiss. Nancy was just wearing her panties, high heels and jewelry, along with her make-up, as she was frantically making the bed. The room had an odor of stale sex.

"Hi, Nancy."

She was not the inhibited type.

"Hi Roland, just running late, had a busy day, you know. I was out early today, didn't even have the time to clean the house, or make the bed. Will need a few more minutes to slip my dress on and get my overnight bag."

Looks like I missed the party, where are your kids?"

"Why the third degree, Roland? Are you accusing me of

something?"

I glanced across the room and noticed an empty glass on each of the side tables. "O, I Just had a friend stop by for a drink or two, you know, just discuss the good old days, share a few laughs. And, the kids wanted to spend the weekend with their father. I can't deny him his kids, so he picked them up yesterday after work. After all! Don't you get to see your daughters whenever you want to Roland? Now tell me how do I look this evening? Tempting? Am I overdressed? Hey, do I fit the bill for your tantric Sutra woman – whatever the fuck it is. Now, Roland, am I overdressed for our special romantic evening, Roland?"

"Your outfit fits you fine, it is all you, Nancy – for sure. Remember, less is more. Though I am a bit confused. You told me you spent last evening with your kids, and this was the reason we could not get away for the weekend?"

"Hey, Roland, I don't have to tell you everything, you know."

"This is true, Nancy, just the truth."

"What does that mean, Roland, another one of your 'Golden Rules?'"

"Would you rather I play by your rules, Nancy?"

"Hey, professor, are you trying to fuck with my head?" She fumed as she stomped to her well-stocked closet to pick out a dress.

She entered the kitchen, dressed to the max. She was rather hot for a 40-something woman, though she would never even tell me her age.

"So do I look sexy now, Roland?"

"Well, to be honest, I think you looked sexier before you put the dress on."

"Ahh, men! It's about the dress, Roland, that makes the woman tempting and seductive, don't you agree?"

"Well, to be honest, Nancy, if that were true, I would take the dress with me to the concert and dinner, and leave you home."

"Roland, always with a quick-witted sarcastic rebuttal. Let's compromise. I will let you take off my clothes when we get to our romantic suite. Why – hell with the stupid blues concert, just drive to the dam hotel. Who the hell is this B.B. King, anyway? Is he as boring as the classical and jazz trash you listen to? Besides, how good could this music be if they call it the blues?"

At the show she looked totally bored. She was focused on an intense texting conversation, or getting up to go to the bar. She finally fell asleep halfway during the show. She seemed to have lost her spontaneity over the past month, and was becoming more withdrawn and prone to argue. She said little on the way to the hotel, made no reference to the show or engaged in small talk.

She was lethargically picking her way through her appetizer, after ordering the most expensive, as well as an expensive entrée. She did not comment on the food. Was indifferent to my presence.

Our waiter then placed a vodka tonic in front of her at our table, "Compliments of the gentleman at the bar, for a fine-looking lady."

After total silence throughout the appetizer course, she came alive as her eyes sparkled. She looked over to the bar, to a short portly middle-aged-looking guy, balding, and with a day's stubble on his oversized jowls. He was wearing worn work boots, jeans, a polo shirt, and a poor excuse for a sport jacket – nothing seemed to match. She raised her glass to him with a toast of thanks as they both smiled at each other. I began to feel more confident in my ill feelings about her, and was now beginning to see the other Nancy I always suspected. She pushed her food away, and told me she had to go to the ladies room, taking her cell phone with her.

"Be right back, Roland, have to make a stop."

"Sure, Nancy, do you ladies now use a cell phone to powder your nose?"

"Another one of your sarcastic academic remarks – I will be right back."

I sat there alone eating, and hoping I would receive a call from anyone to give me an excuse to leave. When the main entrees arrived, Nancy still had not returned. I turned my head around in the direction of the bar, and found Nancy standing next to him. Both had drinks in their hands and were laughing. I left the table to insert myself into their conversation.

"Hey, Nancy, I hate to break up your party, but our dinner is getting cold. It would be appropriate for us to attend to our dinner."

"O Roland, just have the waiter bring the food to the bar, what better way for us to celebrate our special evening than among old friends."

"Well, Nancy, I do not see any of my old friends present. Besides I thought we were celebrating our relationship, not your homecoming party."

"Knock it off, Roland ... hey, bartender, another round of drinks for my friend and me ... place it on the room tab."

"Well, Nancy, that was rather nice of you to order a round of drinks on me, without ordering one for me."

"Always thinking of yourself aren't you, Roland?"

"So, Nancy, are you going to introduce me to your long-lost friend?"

"O forgive me, Roland, this is my old friend, and ummh high school sweetheart – Sal. We go back a long way together."

"Hey Sal this is my new beau. Aren't I a lucky woman ... his name is Roland."

The bartender returned with their drinks.

"Hey, Sal, I am sure you are happy for Nancy. Why don't you make a toast to our special evening?"

"O ungracious me, listen everyone, a special toast to me and this fine and charming woman I have known since grade school."

Those around the bar applauded the toast, as Nancy gave Sal a kiss and hug.

"Why Roland, isn't Sal so gracious and such a handsome gentleman."

As Nancy and Sal turned their backs on me to watch the televised football game, Nancy commented to me, "Sal is so knowledgeable, and up on sports, he has a lot riding on the games tonight – we may both win big tonight? Isn't he so exciting?"

Sal then turned to me and asked, "Hey Roli, why aren't you drinking and getting shit-faced like the rest of us. O sorry, Roli, you back on the wagon or something? Don't be ashamed to tell me. Why I have been on and off the wagon all my life. How about you, Roli, how long you been on the wagon? Like man, you got discipline – how long has it been, Roli?"

"About 53 years."

"Fifty-three years, when the fuck did you start drinking? In your mother's womb? Either that or you are well preserved for a 75-year-old man. So when did you stop drinking Roli, what's your secret?"

"Well, I never started – Sali! And my name is Roland."

"Well lookey here, Mr. Prim and Proper – don't get so touchy and bent out of shape about your name, Roli! Why? What the fuck kind of name is Roland anyway?"

"Well Sali, I am having a hard time believing you never heard this name before?"

"It's Sal … not Sali … OK, you got that right man?"

"Sali, you are being far too sensitive now."

"Why all you fucking liberal professors are all fucking communists, and probably gay. So, Roli, why do you wear your hair long at your age? Waiting for another Woodstock reunion?"

"I choose to wear my hair long for the same reason you are bald at your age! Why, Sali, you don't look a day over 65! And, I am as gay as you are intelligent. And by the way, how do you know I am a professor, Sali?"

"Well, uummhhh, you look like one."

"What line of work you in Sali?"

Why, I own my own plumbing business. Here is my card, Roli."

"Interesting name, The Village Plumber – Flush with experience."

"Yeah, I am a master plumber with a license, Roli. So how long have you been teaching at Barrett College? Hey, is it true that you professors fuck all the hot girls on campus for a good grade?"

"How do you know I teach at Barrett College, Sali? I just met you."

"Just a guess, my friend."

"Hey, bartender, another drink for my friend Sali – make sure its Grey Goose, only the best for my friend Sali"

"Hey, Roli, how did you know this is my favorite brand of vodka?"

"Well, you know, it's Nancy's favorite as well, and I do not believe she is a two-fisted drinker. And figuring you are friends and drinking partners ... and ummmhhh, and former lovers. Tell me, Sali, do you see Nancy often?"

"Why do you ask, Roland? You the jealous type, Roland?"

"No – just no man's fool."

"Well isn't that a lot of bravado coming from Mr. Soft Hands?

"Well, not as often as you shit-eating plumbers fuck other men's women."

"Hey man – back off – Roli, what you are implying, but hey, don't get bent out of shape just because I am having a little fun with your woman."

Sali was drunk by now, unable to control his conversations – liquor makes for a loose tongue, one I would easily exploit.

"So, Sali, you and Nancy seem to have a real affinity for one another, what's the story? You two still have deep feelings for one another. No problem Sali, I don't encroach on another man's turf."

"Hey, Roli, just fuck off with all this lamenting. Just have a few drinks and loosen up. After all, what do you expect from Nancy and me? We were married to each other a long time ago. It was our first marriage for both of us … you know … being young and stupid … comprendo, Professor Roli?"

"Well, it is better than being old, drunk and stupid."

"Go fuck yourself, Roli! As a divorced man you tellin me you never cozy up with your ex for some little fun for old times' sake."

"Why would I want to cozy up with someone I paid a small fortune to get out of my life, and have nothing of old times' sakes to be happy about?"

"Why you never dropped in on Barbara for a surprise quickie?"

"So, how do you know my ex's name? Only Nancy would have known this."

"Ummhh ummhhh, hey man, you trying to fuck with my brain, Roli?"

"I can't fuck with something you don't possess, Sali!"

"So, Sali, old boy, when were you married to Nancy, and when did you guys get divorced?"

Sali was now so inebriated, his tongue was loose, revealing secrets.

"Bartender, vodka, straight up for my new friend – make it Grey Goose!"

"Why, Roli, I had you all wrong, man ... thanks. The bartender placed the shot in front of him. Sal raised it for a toast.

"To my new friend, Roli ... O, I mean ... Dr. Roli ... cheers!" He slapped me on the back.

"Hey, Sali, now I get it, so you and Nancy were married young. Then what happened?"

"Well, Roli, we were not good for each other, you know, both being alcoholics. Trying to keep our demons down. We were only married a few years. We decided to break clean. Start all over. I figured she could do better. Find a guy with direction and goals ... like some gentleman professor ... or professional who knows how to treat women."

"So what happened next, Sali?"

"Well, she got her act together, cleaned herself up, and went back for her GED. So she could get a job to support herself. I was always falling off the wagon, and was of no help to her. She found a job as a receptionist for a local accounting firm, working her way up to the office manager. That is where she met her second husband. He was a little older, and Nancy is always easy to look at; she wasted little time in wooing him away from his wife. He fell head over heels for her, divorced his wife, married Nancy, and they had two children together."

"Bartender, another round for my new friend. So what happened next, Sali?"

"Her old demons kept knocking on her door, she could not keep them down – runs in her family."

I looked to see where Nancy was. She was now sitting next to some other guy engaged in a deep conversation, rather blue collar, local redneck type.

"So what happened next, Sali?"

"Well, he finally had enough and divorced her, with Nancy making out like a bandit, got the house, alimony and child support." She moved on to another job, cleaned up her act, and was doing really good keeping her demons down. Then she received the notice a few months ago that broke her."

"What notice, Sali?"

"Well, didn't Nancy tell you her house is in foreclosure, and she is being evicted by the end of the month? Poor Nancy, she is so self-destructive when she invites her demons in. I tried helping her, throwing her a grand or two when I hit big – it just was not enough to keep her afloat."

"Afloat? She told me how much she gets from her ex each month, and she working as well. How can her house be in foreclosure, she is making out better than most people I know, Sali – what's her story?"

I glanced over to Nancy, she had her arm around the guy she was talking to, laughing as she emptied another glass.

"So go on, Sali."

"Well, you know, she stops taking her medications, for her ups and downs, she lets her demons in all at once."

"What demons, Sali"? "Well, her drinking, gambling, and sex addictions – she gambled away all her income, is losing everything. Even her kids – the husband won custody of the kids, and she lost her job."

"Bartender, get my good friend here a strong coffee, he has had enough, no more drinks for him – OK. He is a danger to himself and society if he gets behind the wheel."

I walked Sali to sit him down in the lounge.

"Hey, Sali, you have been most helpful and insightful. Where are the keys to your car?"

"I left them under the driver's floor mat in my truck."

"Thanks, Sali."

By now he was shit-faced, and oblivious, too drunk to know who he was talking to.

"So, Sali, looks like you and Nancy had a lot to celebrate today, you know, bumping into her by accident this evening at the bar. Looks like you made each other happy ... uuhhhhh?"

"Hey, man-to-man, you know, I was having some fun with ya before. You know, guys just bonding at the bar. Hey, let's talk real guy stuff, she is hot when she gets drunk man. Why, when she called me all upset and crying today, looking for a little support, needed a little affection you know, I figure hey it's kind of erotic fucking my ex-wife before her boyfriend comes over. You know, she gives some great head and tail. Why that lucky dog, she is really into some kinky shit, man".

"So, Sali, did Nancy feel guilty cheating on her new boyfriend?"

"Shhhhhuuu ... don't talk too loud – her boyfriend, Dr. Roland, is at the bar." "O fuck that wuss! He's no man, what she sees in him is beyond me. White-collar trash". "Nancy isn't into that fidelity shit you know – Hey, you isn't a friend of that communist sissy professor boyfriend of hers are you?"

"No way, man, I don't know that dumb naïf. Sali, do you have something against professors or the white-collar professional-type guys? I mean, to do a guy's woman before a date is outright cold, breaks the gentleman's code, you know."

Her philosophy is what he don't know won't hurt him – only benefits me. She was down on her luck, she was desperate. So I threw her a quick three grand ... in return for a tumble or two. It was worth it ... Easy money for both of us – had a good day at the races. By the way ... what's your name again, I can't remember ever seeing you before ..."

O, I am sorry, please forgive my rudeness – its Charlie, but that's not important now. You stay put here til you sober up, OK?"

"Where ya going, Charlie, I owe you something for all your kindness."

"O, Sali, the pleasure is all mine, you already compensated me handsomely."

"Hey Charlie, I feel bad, man. I have a confession to make. You seem like a real guy. I never told no guy this before, but I do feel guilty for fucking my ex-wife before her professor beau came over. It was pure payback – jealous rage."

"Sali you can tell me, I am your friend. I am here to help you. What is your story? I can help you."

"Well, you see, Charlie, I was madly in love with Nancy, we were high school sweethearts, and we married young. I thought she really loved me, Charlie. Then one day I came home early to surprise her with flowers, only to find her in bed with some sissy white-collar accountant. She left me to marry him – I got it, what would she want with a shit-smelling dumb plumber like me. I isn't no rocket scientist, no worldly guy, just a plumber with a GED. Since that day, I developed a hatred for teachers, gentleman, professionals and white-collar trash. I just wanted to get back at them all through that dam fucking Roli guy. When Nancy said they were coming here tonight, I just made it my point to come here and humiliate him in public, knowing I just fucked his girlfriend.

Hey, Charlie, I am really a bad person … isn't I man? I owe that Roli fella a real apology, come clean. I know he will never forgive me and leave Nancy in a lurch. If he leaves her, she will never recover. She has nothing to live for. Hey, Charlie, you think that Roli guy will forgive me?"

"Hey, Sali, that was a heartfelt confession, I am sure he has already forgiven you, and is most grateful for having met you. Now you just sit here, OK? I am going to get you to your room."

"Hey, Charlie, now ease my mind. I was honest and open with you man-to-man, and confessed my guilt. I carry a great pain. In our younger days, Nancy and I believed we could wash away our sins with a drink in hand. Now I am very remorseful. Now, Charlie, my friend ... tell me man-to-man ... look me in the eye ... you ever fuck another man's wife? Be honest. I don't want to burn alone in hell. I isn't no angel Charlie, though I'm a God-fearing man. Why, I was on the wagon for years, doing well, making good money, being a loving husband and father. Then I went to see Nancy after she called me in panic. She was suicidal. I had my reservations about going ... you know ... only fools and sinners repeat the same mortal sins. Thou shall not covet thy neighbor's wife. I felt so guilty afterward about what I did to that poor guy Roli. He's a genuine guy. How could I be such a fool to drink from the same passion well twice? Once I realized what I did to an innocent guy, I thought I could wash this sin away too with a drink. Not even with a bottle of the best vodka. So, Charlie, tell me for my own peace of mind ... answer me – you ever fuck another man's wife?"

I just froze in my own guilt.

"Hey, Sali, 'Let him who is without sin cast the first stone.' Sali, I promise, I will throw not a single stone at you. Now you just stay put. Your sincerity is your redemption, Sali. I will have Nancy take care of you; I am sure you will need each other now. Now you just stay put. Just think of all she can do for you."

"Hey, Charlie, here's my card. Next time you're in town give me a call; we can go have a few drinks together." "

OK, Sali. I promise"

I walked back to the bar. Nancy was talking to the bartender, the place was now empty and closing.

"Hey, Nancy."

Her dinner was still in front of her untouched, she was shit-faced, the bartender refused to serve her any more drinks.

"Hey Nancy, how ya holding up?"

As she got up she had a hard time standing, and could hardly walk.

"Hey, Roolaaand," as she slurred every word. "What time is it? Hey, we goooing to celebrate tonight? Hold me steady, Roland. Can you help me to our romantic suite?"

"Sure, honey, it is right this way. I got you, don't worry, you are in good hands."

I walked her to our suite and placed her on the bed.

"O, could you go to the car and bring me my suitcase, in the meantime I will be waiting for you. Feel free to restrain me if I become too wild. Are you going to give me a lesson ... professor? Make me your whore? Now you will get the real me ... ummmh hurry back now. It's our special night. I can't wait till I move in with you so I can have you on my side every night."

She threw me a kiss as I left the room. By the time I returned with her suitcase she was fast asleep and snoring, sprawled out spread eagle and naked on the bed, with an empty champagne bottle in one hand.

I just looked at her beautiful body with apathy. I did not see a sexy woman, amorous, wanting to make love to the fullness, having all her senses aroused with extended foreplay in the tradition of the *Kama Sutra*. Her flesh was numb like her inebriated soul. I always approached lovemaking from the deep interiors of my soul. It is through the soul that one reaches the higher degrees of ecstasy. Even as a teenager, I would not get a girl drunk just to fuck her for my own personal pleasure. Believing if she did not remember – you were persona non grata as her lover. I am not a proponent of solo sex. Nor desired or engaged in backseat quickies. In my youth I learned to enjoy real lovemaking and to extend the joy as long as possible. One can only satisfy himself when he has satisfied his lover. True love is only achieved when the flesh and soul orgasm as one. I am sure a lesser man would not have turned down this enticing sight. The better man never lowers himself to necrophilia. I find no reason or pleasure in reducing lovemaking to date rape with my partner.

I threw a blanket over her, left her a Dear Jane letter in an envelope on the dresser, and turned off the light as I left. I walked to Sali's van in the parking lot and found his keys under the floor mat and walked back to the hotel. As I approached the front door I saw Sali staggering looking for the men's room – having already soiled himself. I walked over to the night manager to turn the keys over to him, to be returned to Sali when he sobered up. I walked him over to Nancy's room.

"Hey, Sali, it's best you stay off the road tonight for your sake and the general public's, so I arranged a room for you."

I escorted him to the door, telling him he needed to get some sleep. He was too drunk even to hear me. I closed the door and never looked back. I paid for the room, along with the tab for all the rounds of drinks at the bar and for breakfast in bed for two – the price was worth the escape.

> *"Happy is the man who has broken the chains which hurt his mind,*
> *and has given up worrying once and for all."*
> - Ovid, *Metamorphoses*

Dinner for One

I headed south on Route 9 reflecting on the evening's events, with a sigh of relief. I felt relieved, free and confident that my feeling about Nancy was correct. The last thing I needed in life was another relationship with a woman with severe mental disorders. All in all, it was an expensive night, though it was well worth it – escaping another personal disaster. I got away clean, no drama or regrets. There truly are 50 ways to leave a lover.

I reflected on the good position I found myself in as I entered the autumn of my life. My business was doing well, I was teaching at a few colleges – though I lost my long-standing adjunct position at Saint Thomas University – my artwork was in good demand, commanding generous commissions. I was enjoying a good social life with a lot of friends, was composing songs, playing out at a lot of local blues clubs, and after a few years of neglect, I was finally getting back into my spiritual work, as I entered the next phase of the Great Work.

I began to amuse myself with my typical critical self-effacing thoughts. I laughed at myself – even mockingly – at the irony of this evening's events. Here was my girlfriend – pushing me for a commitment, while she was having an affair with her ex-husband, who was paying her to have sex so she could pay off her gambling debts. Believing I would never find out. Then to see them both feeling their guilt, as they got themselves drunk to wash away their sins, while they were both falling off the wagon together! ... And, here I am, a divorced God-fearing man, ex-Catholic, now an apostate Mormon, having fallen off the wagon by drinking my devil's brew of coffee? Making plans to see a woman I had an adulterous affair with? The frail human condition. Am I the cause or the victim?

What choices did I really have last night? How else could I have ended it? I reflected, I just could not see myself having sex with a naked corpse, knowing she just had sex with her libertine husband … heaven knows whether he has any diseases. Should I have requested a STD test from Nancy? The evening could not have gone better if it were a script from a play. Then, getting my comeuppance by getting her ex drunk to make his admission of guilt. Bravo – even if I have to say so myself. Then have them both wake up in the morning in bed not knowing what had happened. I would love to be a fly on the wall for that scene. I just counted my blessings. Amen.

It was a beautiful fall evening, I lost consciousness of time and location by the time I pulled myself out of my reflective reverie, finding myself in Fishkill – it was around 2 a.m. I pulled into the 24-hour Arcade Dinner, and was easily seated at a booth of my choice. I ordered a coffee – anathema for Mormons – joining Sali and Nancy in falling off the wagon. I stared out the window for some inspiration, only to catch a glimpse of my tarnished reflection.

I began writing down a few notes, made a few journal entries, checked my messages and e-mails, and scratched out a few lyrics for a new song or two, as I contemplated my upcoming dinner date with my muse, paramour and mutual adulterer. In one respect I was happy to see her, and glad she reached out to me – I never thought she would call me again – I had simply relegated her to a poem and a song. We did not leave each other on the best of terms. In another respect, I had strong doubts whether I would be able to restrain myself from getting involved with her again. I still carried a lot of guilt for having an affair with a former student and married woman. And, more importantly, how I had corrupted her innocence. Another man would not have thought twice about his conquest, and would have slept quite well each night just dreaming about his lustful affair.

What could be so important about her urgency to see me, and for my benefit not hers? Was she pregnant? Did she carry my child? My thoughts vacillated between the heaven and hell I created for myself. Was I any better than Nancy or Sali? My self-doubt and guilt were waging a bitter war for the dominance of my condemned soul.

Life is nothing more than a series of absurd contradictions that lead us on an arduous path of uncertainty, bad choices and regrets. One must embrace his absurdities before one can revolt against them – it is our amor fati.

She was a former student, enrolled in my Economics of Social Issues course at Saint Thomas University. To be honest, I was never sure which Saint Thomas it was named for, Saint Thomas Aquinas or Saint Thomas the doubter. I was beginning to doubt both of them. Here I was teaching the Economics of Social Issues, as a conservative Mormon lecturing at a liberal Catholic University. It was like awarding the Nobel Peace Prize to ISIS.

I could not stop thinking of her. She was a tall, Midwestern all-American girl. Born and bred in Idaho with traditional values and genuine old-fashioned manners. Blond, blue-eyed, with Nordic facial features and skin like peaches and cream. She had a stunning figure, carrying herself with grace and dignity, and only her sincerity and humility surpassed her beauty. As a strict rule, I never get involved with students or with women almost half by age – and never with married women. I always had the self-discipline and wisdom, along with good character to know better, and to avoid such delusions of folly. She was as young as my youngest daughter, and married. She held a strong grip on my soul – with a magic spell to make me fall for her – from heaven's graces into a hell of love.

Fidelity is a double-edged sword; all relationships covet it, though few have the restraint to practice it; for years I was one of those monogamous romantics who learned the hard lesson that fidelity is a zero-sum game if only one partner is participating. It is an emotional Russian roulette played with a single bullet of temptation. Once you start the game, the bullet of temptation will strike your heart while killing your soul. My existential mind was now in conflict with my seeking soul for dominance over my next course of decisions, and actions they would breed. I was caught between my daydreams of a middle-aged man, and the nightmare of truth I must confront. I was wise enough to know that virtue with a disciplined morality are good for the soul – though painful on the heart. Either choice I elected would curse me to a life of regrets. Regretfully, there is no common ground or compromise – it's a choice between sin and grace.

By the time I pulled my thoughts together and left the diner, it was dawn. I finally called it a night and headed home. Her memories were now whispering to me, sprouting like seeds in my restless heart.

Whispers

The night whispered memories
Of her muted name
Her fair northern skin
Was as clear as the blue sky

She walked oblivious to her beauty
Though no stranger to men
Her smile radiated the dawn
Breaking the dark night of my soul within

She hid under her umbrella of passions
Always speaking from the heart
With words never said
She was a light ... burning true
Her genuine soul... was well read

She danced with pennies in her eyes
To hide her golden heart
She exposed herself to my mystery
Never casting doubt
She stirred by soul about

Roland, 5:18 a.m.

The Wakeup Call

I was awoken from my sound and peaceful sleep around 1 p.m. by an incessant doorbell. I ignored it as long as I could, believing it was the Jehovah's Witnesses canvassing the neighborhood. The ringing was then supplemented by a pounding on the door, and a woman calling my name. When I finally dressed and opened the door, I found Nancy at the door disheveled with that hangover look on her face. Sali was in his idling truck in the parking lot.

"Roland, please, we need to talk, I can explain everything. I am sure you are mature enough to listen to me and work with me to straighten this silly little incident out – and get back with our lives."

"Well, Nancy, wait here at the door and I will get you your personal belongings. Then you can leave."

"Roland, just let me in and give me a few minutes to explain."

"Wait here, Nancy, I am sure you do not want to keep your ex-husband and paramour waiting?"

"Just let me explain, Roland."

"Nancy, you lied to me and cheated on me. There is nothing you can say to save this relationship! It's over, Nancy."

"Roland, please, I will get help, I will go for therapy, sign myself into a rehab center."

"Nancy, it is over, just listen to yourself, you did not once say you were sorry."

"Fuck you, Roland! Always thinking of yourself! What's the

matter Roland – can't take the competition?"

"You are so right, Nancy, there are more bars, barstools and men for you to pursue. I do not compete in your world of bar morality. I do wish you the best."

"Roland! Roland! Please listen to me, please!"

"Well, Nancy, once again you gambled, and bet on the wrong horse. Besides, you are better suited for a mule."

"Roland … Roland! It was just an innocent indiscretion."

"Nancy, at your age, you should be wise enough to know we can't control the aging process. We get old, wrinkled and ugly. What we can control is our character and morals. At this stage of our lives good people look for these qualities in a relationship – knowing full well we have little say in our physical decline. Why would I chose a woman like you – knowing in a few years your beauty will decline and you have no character or commitment to fidelity to a relationship. If you were honest with yourself when you look into the mirror every morning, you would see there are more wrinkles in your cheating and lying soul then on your face."

"Well, Roland, why I never looked at it this way … well, I never saw it this way before. All my friends said I should just have a good time for myself, and if you don't get caught … it's not cheating."

"Nancy, well, this is something for you to contemplate in the future when you are all alone at a bar on a Saturday night. Was your affair with your ex-husband worth the loss of our relationship?"

"Hell, Roland, you can't control me!"

"You are so right, Nancy, this is why I am setting you free."

"O, Roland, I hate you and your high standards; you can't expect me to live by your rules."

"Right again, Nancy, here are your belongings, you are now

free to live by your standards."

"Roland, please, I have nowhere to go. What about my kids?"

"Take them to the bar with you and Sali."

I gave Nancy her belongings and closed the door.

I spent the rest of the day grading papers, teaching myself how to play the lute, and writing a few reflective metaphysical poems. I was at peace now, knowing the truth, and being able to complete my work without the profane drama. For good relationships should not allow room for doubt or competition. This is what Nancy was all about. Overall, it was a beautiful day – the perfect autumn in full shimmering color. I retired early to bed, alone, and in hope of a peaceful sleep free of the reoccurring nightmares I had been experiencing over the last few weeks.

Contemplation

My sleep was again interrupted by the same nightmare, though this one more intense and very clear. I awoke from my sleep screaming out in fear and doubt. I could not fall back to sleep. I went to my meditation room to recite a few prayers and rituals. I then just readied myself for the day ahead, showered and dressed, then left my loft. My schedule was open for the day, except for a 10:30 a.m. Business Ethics course at Barrett College, filling my morning till noon. After class I headed to one of my favorite haunts, Karen's Kitchen in Cold Spring, to enjoy a cup of organic coffee al fresco overlooking the Hudson. I had plenty of time on my hands, affording me the pleasure to reminisce about how my past affair with a married woman still haunts me today. Where was the line that marked my transition from being her guardian angel to a tempting demon?

My thoughts drifted back to when she first caught my eye. Her beauty and sweet demeanor were eminent, though she was not in the least bit a temptress. She was an anachronism – though timeless, a well-placed contradiction never to be challenged, though always accepted. It was almost as if she was oblivious to her natural beauty. Her old-time traditional Midwestern upbringing and values preempted such behavior. She stood out among all the other women in the class. She was far from vain, always smiling – though far too innocent and quite naive to see the jealousy of the other women in class who frowned when her fellow male students traced her movements into the classroom. Her female classmates were outright cruel with the faces and names they mocked her with behind her back. Especially when she aced every test with ease.

I was most cautious not to call on her in class for participation, knowing well her female classmates would only hate her more for her intelligent responses. And accuse me of bestowing favoritism upon her, not to mention all the rumors that would follow. I never spoke with her one-on-one. Though I do recall overhearing one particular conversation she was having with a few of her male classmates early on in the semester before class. They were obviously charmed by her beauty, and trying to pierce her moral armor for some opportunities. She always wore her wedding band, making her commitment very clear. She was always a gracious diplomat, knowing well how to deflect an unwelcome compliment full of innuendo. I listened as she told her wannabe suitors she would love to join them for a drink after class, but her Methodist faith would not allow it, and she was busy with school work, and planning a surprise birthday party for her loving husband of three years. She was brilliant – a woman who had it all together, and at such an early age. Her maturity surpassed her looks.

The first time I actually spoke to her one-on-one, was the evening of the final exam. She was usually the first to hand in her work, well before the other students. She was unaware she was always raising the bar of her classmates, to their dismay. On this particular evening she was the last to finish, even requesting more time – which I easily granted. I could see there was something troubling her, she was almost unrecognizable without her bright smile that lit her face up like a halo. Finally, she got up, organized her belongings and walked up to my desk.

"Thank you, Professor, for granting me more time to complete my exam, it is very gracious of you. I know it's late and sure you would like to go home – especially this late in the evening."

"No apology required. How do you think you did? Do you believe it was a fair exam, Candice?"

"Most fair, as usual, no objections. You are a most learned, patient and caring academic – quite a rarity."

"That's most kind of you, though a bit overrated. I have to say, you do not look well this evening, are you ill?"

"No professor, just a bad day. Will I have the opportunity to retake the exam, if I do not do well as I would have expected?"

"Sure, Candice, no problem at all. You have my contact info, reach out to me when you are up to it – are you sure you are OK? You look quite distraught."

"Thanks for all your concern, Professor. I really enjoyed your class and learned a lot."

"Thank you, Candice – be well and have a Merry Christmas. Any plans for the holidays?"

She looked at me as her eyes welled up with tears. "Maybe a new direction in life, Professor. Well I have taken enough of your time."

She walked toward the door then stopped, standing there for what appeared to be an eternity. I was not sure how to respond. She walked back to my desk.

"Professor, I am sorry for the inconvenience again. Would it be appropriate if I ask you for some personal advice? I have no family in the area, or trusted friends, and have no place to go home to this evening."

"Please Candice, speak with candor, knowing this will be confidential. Are you in trouble?"

"Yes, but as a victim, not a criminal."

"Candice, please, how may I help?"

"Well, I believed I was happily married to a man I thought I knew, loved and trusted. He is someone I knew since my days in

Idaho. We attended the same high school. When he returned from college, he landed himself a great job as a software engineer with the largest computer manufacturer in town – the world. He was handsome, polite and a gentleman. He courted me, and even proposed to me on his knees. We were engaged, and were soon married. We never engaged in intimacy until marriage. He was a man of good character and old-time fidelity. Shortly after our wedding, he was given a big promotion and transferred to the Hudson Valley. I was so happy for him. He also had family in the area so I felt comfortable leaving the security of my family."

"What happened next, is he alright?"

"Soon after we moved here, his job required long hours. He would leave early in the morning, and not return home till late evening. As time went on he even stopped calling me during the day just to say hello. I would call his family out of concern to inquire what was going on. I was concerned he may have a nervous breakdown or something. On the weekends he would ignore me, and would not spend any time with me. I then took a job, and enrolled in college so I could also make a life for myself. I thought he was just being overwhelmed with his job, and I wanted him to be successful and move up the corporate ladder."

"I left work early today, went to buy a few nice gifts for him, and planned a surprise birthday for him this evening when he arrived home from work after midnight. When I went home today, I saw his car in the driveway, and the door was locked. When I went in, I heard a lot if giggling. I went into the bedroom and caught him in bed with another woman – his boss!"

"When he saw me, he started to yell at me, and asked why I was not at work. I stood there frozen, in disbelief. I finally rallied enough courage to tell his boss to get dressed and get out. I told them I would be back later this evening for my belongings."

"What happened next?"

"He told me it's his house, and he would not let me in, and if I returned it would get ugly, and threatened me with violence."

"What did his bed partner do?"

"She just calmly got dressed, was indifferent, and then told me not to be so selfish and possessive. Then looked at me and said, 'Hey kid, wake up, little girl, this is not Idaho, this is how we live here, poachers take all.'"

I just ran out of the house, and drove around for hours before coming to class. I am sorry, I have no one to turn to. What are my options?"

"What would happen if you went home to get your personal things?"

"I am afraid he won't let me in, or he may get violent. I did manage to take some clothes, and some things. What should I do? I am all alone, no family, or place to stay."

I was quite moved by her peril.

"Well, Candice, I would call the local police to report your situation, inform them he threatened you with violence, and request they meet you at the home to ensure he does not harm you."

"I am in no condition to call the police. I will break down hysterically, and am afraid they won't take me seriously."

"Are there any female students that can assist you?"

"Professor, I know how they talk behind my back, and ignore me, or have something sarcastic to say. I have no one to trust here. All of my friends and family are in Idaho."

"I see, Candice. Well it is getting late, and the night janitors will be arriving soon to shut down the building. With your permission, I will call the police to arrange for them to meet you at the house. I will call a local hotel and reserve a room for you, until such time you can make other arrangements."

"Professor, this is very kind of you, but I am afraid to go there without some form of moral support. I am not in an emotional good place; I just caught my husband in bed with another woman in my house. I am angry, and feel betrayed. I cannot let him see me in such a vulnerable position. Besides, I do not have the money to pay for the rooms. I do not have that line of credit on my card."

"I well understand the pain you are going through – I was once married, and no stranger to the pain of infidelity. I will follow you to your home to meet the police, and be your chaperone. I will follow you to your hotel to ensure you arrive safely. I will also have to notify school security to file a report to have the incident on record, in the event he tries to harass you on campus. I will also have to inform my dean for disclosure to ensure I am not violating any rules of misconduct."

"Thank you, Professor, I will sign any affidavit attesting to your good conduct, and assisting me, so as to not bring suspicion or harm to your good character."

She was most genuine and sincere; I never doubted her good character. I called the police to report the incident, and to request escort service for her. The New York State Police had jurisdiction over the hamlet where she lived, and made the arrangements to meet us there. I called a local hotel to book a room for her for the next few days, until she could make arrangements to go home to be with her family. I also called campus security to file a report for the record. She called her husband to inform him she was coming over to pick up her possessions. I overhead the conversation – her cell was on speaker phone, to have a witness hear his response.

"Candice, I will not allow you in. I will lock the door, and if you try to enter, I will bar your entrance ... do you hear me! Don't force me to do something you will regret! Remember who

Richard Cirulli

you are dealing with!"

When we arrived, the police were already at the scene. Seeing the police in the driveway, her husband started to throw her belongings out the window. His love interest was still there. Candice went to unlock the door with her key, but realized he had changed the locks. The police informed him if he did not open the door they would force it open, and then called for backup. Candice informed the police the woman inside was his boss, and they both work at the East Fishkill campus. With this information in hand, they informed her husband and his lover they would release the report to the local news for broadcast. Such a news release would result in them both losing their jobs, since the company could ill afford such a scandal.

Candice entered the house escorted by the police, and took all the possessions that would fit in our cars. I also identified myself to the police to state my purpose of being there, and my relationship with Candice. I also requested the police to follow us to the hotel, to ensure I had no hidden agenda. They asked for identification, and complied with my request for escort. Once Candice had taken as many of her valuable possessions as she could, including an old Martin guitar her grandfather had given her when she was a child, we drove to the hotel. I checked her in, paying for her room for the next week, helped her unload her belongings and take them to her room, all under police escort.

In the lobby, the police were waiting to complete the report, and to escort her to her room once I left, as I had requested. The police asked us a few questions before leaving. I informed them I had notified Campus Security, and shared the incident report number with them before we left. Candice made it clear to the police I was only her professor, and was assisting her since she had no family in the area, making it clear we were not in any form of friendship or relationship and that I was only trying to

53

help. She wrote me a note attesting that her family would reimburse for the costs I incurred to assist her. She asked the police to include this in the report, to ensure I would not be charged with misconduct by the university, further informing the troopers I handled the situation with much professionalism.

"Thank you, Professor, for all your help, I am deeply grateful for all you have done. I assure you my family will mail you a check to cover the cost. Please give me your personal contact information – I do not want to send the check to the school, it may only raise a flag, and cause you trouble for your good deeds."

I handed her a few of my business cards.

"Well, what are your plans, Candice – will you be alright?"

"Yes, Professor, I will call my family, and make plans to go home for the holidays, and try to sort things out."

"Well, please keep me informed to let me know if everything is alright. Will you be coming back next semester to finish up your degree?"

"Yes, Professor, I will look you up. The best of the holidays to you and your daughters. I am sure you are a good dad."

"The best of the holidays to you and your family, Candice."

We waved each other good-bye. I caught that beautiful smile of hers return before I turned to walk away. I thanked the state troopers, and requested they escort me to my car. He just smiled, wished me a happy holiday, and told me it was not necessary. He presented his card, and advised me to call him if Candice's husband threatened me.

"He will most likely request a copy of the police report, and your name is on it. He is not a stable man. I suspect more than infidelity with this man."

I went home, too riled to go to bed. Not to mention all the pressure to grade the papers, and to have the grades in by the end of the week. I stayed up all night grading papers – the bane of all professors. I picked Candice's paper out of the pile. It had watermarks on it, and her final was not of the quality expected of her. She failed to answer a few questions. I gave her an "A" for the final, and for the semester grade. She had earned it. She was applying to graduate school, and I wanted her to succeed. I just could not add insult to her injury.

She e-mailed me a week later to inform me she was at home with her parents enjoying the holidays, and extended her thanks for all my help in paying for her meals. Her parents sent their warmest regards, as well. She said they would be sending me a check for the costs once their pension checks arrived. She went on to say she would be returning next semester to complete her degree, and would stop by to say hello, also inquiring what courses I would be teaching. I knew she did not come from money, and her parents were humble and honest hard-working with old-time morality and character. I told her to tell her parents not to send the check, and use the money to help pay for the semester's books. She inquired about her grade, requesting if she could retake the final, in light of her circumstances. I replied, "As a steadfast rule, I don't allow my A students to retake their final exams." She sent back an immediate thank-you, saying, "See you next semester." When her parents' check arrived, I did not cash it. I just ripped it in half, and placed it in a file.

Where did I go wrong? When did I cross the line? Was it a mid-life crisis? Was I confronting my mortality in light of my biopsy report? Or was it just pure lust … a demon I never knew I possessed? I should have read the signs more carefully. Did I ignore my deep unconscious, even during my meditation rituals? As a practicing Magnus, did my rituals and talismans fail to guide me past this arduous path? Did my rituals of esoteric Freemasonry fail me also? Had I lost my portal to the light, being blinded by the desires of the flesh? Was this my final test, or a hell I must walk through before freeing myself from the shackles of the profane flesh?

The weeks following this fateful night, brought on propitious signs, ravens appearing at my window. That haunting nightmare kept returning more frequently as it intensified with evermore clarity. All my rituals of Christian Magic, and work with the Kabala could not exorcise me from these night visitors. I now just prayed and performed my rituals with my petitions to be granted Divine Wisdom to interpret the meaning of these nocturnal visions. At first I began to doubt myself, though over the days my intuition grew stronger with conviction and wisdom as my spiritual eye began to open wide. If I only knew what was to follow, I would not have had the spiritual strength to play the Good Samaritan. Maybe God had blinded my eyes in order for me to see my soul. Or did hell lease its demons to attack my soul for assisting a good soul in distress, for bringing a soul out of darkness. Or was her husband the devil himself – hell bent on possessing my soul?

No Good Deed Goes Unpunished

"Give us Barabbas"

After the holidays I received a call from the dean's office to come see him right away regarding my pending tenure. I knew this was not good news. When I arrived at his office I was escorted to the conference room, where the dean, along with his kangaroo court, were in session. I was on trial and not given the courtesy to prepare for Torquemada's Inquisition. His secretary directed me to my seat in the corner. None of the members present greeted me, not even the clergy.

"Professor ... O, I am sorry, Adjunct Professor. I am sure you know the reason for this meeting. There is no need for formal introductions. I am also sure you know everyone present."

"Well, to be honest, John, I am not at all familiar with all the faces in attendance." "Uummh, Roland, this is disturbing, this is a formal hearing. For the record, are you stating you do not know the president of the college, the dean, department chairs, and our university's in-house legal counsel? And, please address me by my proper title Roland, show respect for once."

"Yes, I am a man who respects academic protocol."

Please, Roland, then please extend me the honor and address me as Dr. Ganelon. Now, Roland, don't' interrupt me with your insubordination!"

"Well, then, John! Please tell me what I am allegedly guilty of. What is the charge?"

"Roland, in your presence we have some rather eminent

professors and clergy. Maybe if you attended all of our functions and fundraisers you would be familiar with them."

"My job is to teach my students! Simply that. My evaluations will speak for themselves, both my peer evaluations and student evaluations."

"O, poor Roland, of course you get good student evaluations, by taking them to hotels, paying for their meals, and getting into every female student's pants in exchange for good evaluations. You bring shame to this esteemed university, Roland."

"And you bring lies and hypocrisy to this table, John. Who bought you off?"

"Roland, we have proof that you brought one of your students to a hotel, and lived there for a week for a sex feast. Can you deny that you did not pay for her room?" … ROLAND?"

"Yes, I did to keep her out of harm's way!"

"And yes, Roland, right into your caring, loving arms as a predator, right!"

"Well, John …"

"Dr. Ganelon to you, Roland!"

"Well, JOHN! Maybe the problem is that all of you can't read. The police report makes it very clear. We escorted the student to her home, to take her belongings out of her house from her cheating, adulterous and abusive husband. She had no money, and I paid for her food and shelter so she would have a place to stay. I did not take her to a shit-hole motel or to my apartment. It's all on record, and I disclosed it to Campus Security, the state police – who are witnesses, and made a full report of disclosure to the dean."

"Now, Roland, as a priest, the chancellor of the university and an esteemed theologian on Christian morality, I declare your morals are not compatible with our high Christian values. Maybe you Mormons get praise for fucking every woman you want. But we, as a Catholic university, cannot condone having our male professors having sex with our female student population at will."

"Well, we Mormons do not bear false witness against our neighbors. Do you priests still follow the Ten Commandments, or are you all too busy fucking little boys in the closet?"

"Roland, watch your heretic mouth. You are talking to one of the primates of the church!"

"Yes, forgive me, I am talking to a monkey who still walks on all fours, and who lacks the Christian virtue of truth! Where are you getting your distorted information from? I have also disclosed to the state police and the school the fact that Candice's husband and his girlfriend have been harassing me. Have you addressed this fact?"

"Well, Roland, of course he is harassing you; what do you expect, you had an affair with his wife.'"

"He was caught in bed with his boss, who both work for HAL, the computer behemoth that owns the county."

"Well, Roland, did you see them in bed having an affair?"

"No I did not."

"Then how can you bear false witness against your neighbor, Dr. Mormon?"

"Candice told me."

"O, you poor lustful fool, of course she did, just as a way to cover up her own adulterous affair. Are you so insecure that you need the affection of every piece of ass that gives an ugly fuck like you a second look?"

"Well, John, then who was that woman at the house that evening when the state police arrived?"

"Roland, that was her husband's boss who came to his distress when he found out his wife was having an affair with you."

"That is an outright lie, slander and defamation of character."

"So, Roland, did her parents send you a check to reimburse you for the costs?"

"They sent it, and I ripped it in half. Candice's parents are hard-working blue-collar people now living on pensions and Social Security. I told her I did not help her expecting anything in return,"

"O, noble Dr. Mormon … nothing in return but her ass!"

"John, why do you delude yourself? You're 45 years old, not married, and attend all the functions alone – And, for the record, I do attend your money-grubbing fundraisers – why, John, you probably have never been laid in your life. Besides, what woman would be attracted to a man of your age who still lives with his parents, who finds excitement collecting stamps, and still has acne – have you reached puberty yet? Can't wait to hear your voice change from your current soprano range. And, besides, I also did my research. Candice's husband's lover is also on the committee that approves the generous grants that fill the university's coffers, and the daughter of the dean of the Computer Science Department – the department that receives the lion's share of the grant money. Is this so, or does your Primate deny this? Would you swear to God above and on your defiled frock? You make a whore out of the department chair's daughter, the Primate gets a generous bonus, along with a free mansion to boot. Will his living expenses being paid by the school? So people like Candice's parents have to scrimp and save just to pay for your inflated tuitions … as you pontificate about helping the poor, though give little aid to your students and needy. You attack me as a smoke screen to cover your devilish and nefarious acts, because you lack the morality and the balls to stand up for what is right. You preach about an almighty and all-knowing God who sees all? Do you now believe He does not see through your lies?"

"Roland. You are fired! We will call Security to escort you off the campus."

"No need to call Security, I will be running so fast to exit your hellish domain, they will never catch up to me! You can take your tenure and my classes away from me, but never my integrity. I only request you have the character, and possess a meager amount of decency, not to harass Candice, and to allow her to graduate with distinction."

"O, Roland, you idealistic fool, we get HAL's grant money, Candice's husband gets a hot piece of ass, you fuck his wife's pussy, Candice graduates magna cum laude, we get rid of you. And we tell the students to believe in a God we deny and mock. Money is the god that blesses us and condemns you, Roland. So where is your God now, Roland?"

I received an email from Candice after the holiday saying she had returned to campus, and to her dismay was informed I was no longer at the university. She further went on to say how happy she was having been able to work things out with her husband. She told me that the Primate of the church and university personally called her upon reading the police and Security reports, and wanted to assist her in any way.

"He went so far as to invite me to the Chancellor's office, to talk to me about how God expects all his children to have the heart to forgive. I was so moved. He said he spoke with my husband and was able to get him into counseling and rehab for his drug and sex addictions. He told me the pressure of his job was so overwhelming that it caused his breakdown, and he went on to inform me I will be giving the commencement speech, and graduating valedictorian, for my perfect 4.0 average. He even wants me to apply to their graduate program, and will give me financial assistance, because my hubby was able to get a big grant from his employer for the business department," Candice's email had said.

"Can you believe this, Professor? All this for a poor old country girl from Idaho. When I inquired about your departure, the dean, Dr. Ganelon, said he was saddened by the news of your departure, but said the school's liberal views of helping the needy and fighting corporate corruption were at odds with your agnostic views, and having no soul or love for humanity. Though, I found that odd. I told Dr. Ganelon I do not remember you this way at all, nor were your lectures ever presented in that vein. He also said you had some personal issues since divorcing your wife for catching her in an affair with her boss. He said you did not have the Christian virtue to forgive. O well, Professor, I really learned a lot from you, and you have truly inspired me. I hope you can attend my graduation."

She was so naive, unaware she was just a pawn in a big cover-up. The computer giant did not want the bad press of having her husband's affair exposed, along with his addictions … not to mention the paybacks and money laundering, which would launch a probe into the conflict of interests, and the meandering pipeline of the grant money. All the players received a nice piece of the never-ending grant money. These bastards were unscrupulous enough to use Candice's innocence and trust against her, without mercy or conscience, and continued to conspire and manipulate her to their advantage … right in front of her face. The grant money would continue to flow from the computer giant to the university's coffers as long as the dean's daughter was kept satisfied in her unending sexual hunger by her paramour sex-addict partner.

It was propaganda at its best, orchestrated by those who propagate the "faith." Candice's husband was instructed to join a local church and get active in the parish. The local media would run stories on how her husband was now born again, and confessed his previous life of sin as an adulterer and cocaine addict. They moved them into a new, bigger home, at a much reduced interest rate because the original loan had been foreclosed on before the house was built. He spoke at women's groups, lamenting and repenting for all his cheating ways, and expounding on how he was now filled with God's Holy Spirit.

The ruse worked. Women no longer viewed him as a womanizer, but a victim of the times, truly repentant for his sins. A man now dedicated to his wife so she might have the best, who was tempted in his time of weakness by the devil with women and drugs. His parish now had a community hall built by an unknown generous sponsor for holding meetings for those with addictions. He and Candice were photographed by the local media holding hands, attending local functions, celebrating anniversaries and birthdays. Candice was placed on local boards, unaware that every time her husband left to attend his fellowship meeting he was whisked away in a limo to a secret location, to be supplied with cocaine and the dean's daughter. As long as he could fill her vagina, HAL would fill the university's coffers. It was a sweet deal.

The probing press was kept away from the police reports, and I was being blackballed, eventually losing all of my teaching positions – even with the best of evaluations from a few surrounding schools. As the heat was put on me, my friends melted away like snow in July. Many of them were bestowed with some rather lucrative no-show contracts, or teaching assignments.

As I walked deeper into my past memories of this event, I was feeling many mixed emotions. I was not sure if I was mad at her, her husband, or myself for playing the role of the white knight in shining armor – or a fool. After all, my chivalrous deed cost me teaching jobs and my credibility. I often wondered – did she set me up? Aside from my existential and psychological self-analysis, in reality it did not matter. We found ourselves as each other's unknowingly victims of time and circumstance. As I traveled back to the foreign country of the past, I found myself a stranger to the present. I could not withdraw from this mental journey of the past; it possessed and followed me now, as I followed it into a future that did not exist.

I felt compelled to run from her, as I felt equally obsessed to see her again. Why would she insist this reunion was more for my benefit than hers? My only benefit was the small consolation that I had helped a student in need. Then haphazardly fell into an illicit affair with her. Unlike my quick and drama-less break-up with Nancy, this break-up had now lingered for over a year of personal trials and tribulations. I only found an uneasy peace by accepting my fall as my penance … assuming it would be less torturous than purgatory, if I made it that far up Jacob's ladder.

I did not hear from her for some time, aside from her invitation to attend her graduation speech. I could not in good conscience set foot on that devil's den of a campus. And what monetary gift could I send her, now that she was living the high life? I just sent her a card wishing her the best.

In frustration and disillusionment, I entered my evening's journal entry:

For What?

Do I extend my hand of fellowship?
Only to receive a fist of anger?

Do I only open my heart to speak truth?
Only to be mocked by the malicious and profane tongue?

64

Do I offer the wisdom of my soul?
Only to be reviled as an interloper?

Do I lend a smile of hope to those in despair?
Only to be returned with a sneer of hate?

Do I cast a sympathetic eye upon the needy?
Only to have them cast a tear upon me?

The Landing

A gentle breeze disturbed her thick hair
Brushing it gently against her innocent complacent face
Like ripples in a once tranquil pond it cast rings about her daydream

In her little annoyance
I saw a hidden composed beauty
That only silent … and unsuspecting eyes could comprehend
A distance apart … though not far
Seemed like an eternity near
Til time ebbed in the thunder
Of a single heartbeat

Unnoticed to my eyes and thoughts
She was oblivious to my presence
We passed each other within our own daydreams
Her subtle graces of movement
Reflected a subdued hidden conscious
In a thought soon to be lost

A tranquil tree-lined garden shades my emotions
Never to be loved
Yet lingers on like the scent of a rose
No longer in my sight

Roland

It was not until the October following her graduation when I received an urgent text, and e-mail from her – tagged high priority – for me to pick her up at Stewart Airport. She was returning to the area from their winter home in Florida. It looked like she had fully accepted her new life, unaware she was a puppet whose strings were being pulled by the chancellor and his henchman, for her to act out her role as the figurehead wife of a repentant sinner. Though at the time, I too was unaware that I was thrown under the martyr's bus by the Machiavellian Primate and his diabolical henchman Dr. Ganelon.

I did return her text, agreeing to meet her at the airport. It was a beautiful autumn day, just like it was almost a year ago to the day. When I met her at the arrival gate, I was expecting to see the bright-eyed smiling Candice that graced the local media over the last year or so. Instead, I saw a saddened and wet-eyed Candice, just like the last time when I left her at the hotel. She looked shaken, even though dressed to the nines, with manicured hair. One remarkable new feature of was her look of maturity, and how she carried herself. She was still the stunning beauty from Idaho, now complete with an aura of womanhood that trumped her college days' cute-girl look. She smiled at me when we made eye contact.

"Hello, Roland, thank you again for being my guardian angel. She gave me a rather long hug, refusing to let go. Then sighed a relief, kissed me on the cheek. We went to reclaim her baggage – she was not traveling light – and I helped carry her baggage to my car."

As we drove away she broke the ice with a compliment … or flattery … depending on one's definition.

"Well, Roland, you never age, you look well. How has life been treating you? One of these days soon you have to tell me what happened to you at Saint Thomas University, everyone there is so hush, hush. Though the rumor is you had an illicit affair with one of your students. I am having trouble believing this; it can't be true! Right, Roland?"

"Well Candice, if it were, I would like to meet this woman who had brought ruin to my life."

"Just what I thought, Roland, and please skip the formalities, everyone just calls me Candy. Roland, I know you are a man of good character; all the women in class were rather impressed with your restraint, and how you always deflected their flirting, and how you always held to those old-time morals. Though I must confess, a few of the women in your class thought you were sexy … hahaha … having to settle with having sex with that weird philosophy professor. Can't remember his name, Roland – he was the defrocked priest. I heard the chancellor paid his female students good hush money, and better grades, in exchange for silence."

"Well Candice, I never had sex with any of my students, never hit on them, nor was there ever a charge of misconduct brought against me."

"What happened Roland? Will you tell me?"

"The tenure committee accused me of taking you to a hotel to have sex with you on the night you found your husband in bed with his love interest."

"That's not true, Roland, at all, I even went to the chancellor personally to tell him all the good things you did, and how moral and compassionate a person you are. Now that I think about it, Roland, he was very indifferent about it, even had a Cheshire cat's smile on his huge jowl face. All he kept talking to me about was to not file a domestic violence charge against my husband. He said it would not be good for the school's stellar reputation, and it may greatly hinder my chances of graduating and being accepted in the graduate program, along with possible loss of job opportunities for being a whistle blower. Roland, something seems amiss, do you know more about this, then you are letting on?"

"I wish I knew more, Candy, it is an enigma to me, and I am still trying to put the pieces together."

"So where am I taking you, Candy?"

"I am not sure, Roland. Can we go someplace to talk, a quiet and private restaurant? Once again, I need your advice and sincere help, to see if I made the right decision. Any suggestions Roland?"

"One of my favorite places is Karen's Kitchen in Cold Spring, a nice artist-like coffee shop that serves organic food and great coffee. It overlooks the Hudson, and they have al fresco seating. I have been going there a lot lately. I used to go there to contemplate, and ponder my decision to divorce my wife. The place brings back so many memories; it seems to be the place where I go to make my big life decisions. They know me there, so we can secure a quiet table not in earshot of eavesdroppers. And, besides, it is out of range of the Poughkeepsie crowd."

When we arrived they obliged my request for a quiet distant table. Candy was quite caught up with the village's charm, and the beauty of the Hudson, along with the fall foliage starting to bloom. She also liked the menu offering organic foods, reminding her of Idaho.

"So, Roland, you are a moral man, and one to be trusted.

After I caught my husband having the affair with his boss, HAL Inc. and the university did all they could to keep the incident silent. They brought in counselors to talk with us, mostly me. They apologized for having placed far too many demands on my husband, because they were so impressed with his work and drive – they lost sight of what the consequences would be. They told me it was unfortunate that he got involved with his boss, but said it was not untypical when female and male work long hours together, away from their loving spouses. They told me they were having his boss transferred to their office in Atlanta. His company also paid in full for all his counseling, and his rehabilitation time at Beacon House – the esteemed treatment center for drug and alcohol abuse, and sex addictions. Why, they even paid him his full salary when on medical leave, citing that they felt responsible for bringing on this condition. I agreed to attend marriage counseling sessions with my husband, believing he was sincere, and loved me."

"What happened next, Candy?"

"Well, when he told me he was going to Florida to close on our winter home, it looked like all was well, and the past was well behind us. He informed me he would close on the house on Monday, and make all the preparations to furnish the house, so he could surprise me on Saturday when I was scheduled to join him. I was quite excited; it looked like he had rid himself of all his demons. So I wanted to surprise him, as well. I went out and bought some rather seductive fine-laced intimate apparel, not to mention lotions and … well I said too much! Since he had overcome his sex addiction, I thought I would reward him. And to ensure him no woman could entice him but me.

"Being a simple country girl, with a puritanical upbringing, I thought maybe I was the problem. You know, I was a virgin when I met my husband, and remained so until our honeymoon

69

night. I was so inexperienced. So feeling guilty and wanting to please him, I read The *Kama Sutra* ... a few times, and had all these fantasies I wanted to explore. So I headed down there a few days early to surprise him. When I arrived, there were two cars in the driveway, and I found the front door open – the house was empty and quiet. So I showered, and made myself ready, lit a few candles, and lit some incense. Then closed my eyes thinking, 'Wait til he sees this ... just what he always wanted.' I could not wait to see his reaction when he walked into the bedroom seeing me in bed, lying in wait like a hungry lioness.

"Next I heard some laughter, and giggles, then the door slam. They both walked in naked, and drying themselves off, kissing and groping each other, unaware of my presence. When they walked into the room, I saw it was the same woman from before – his boss! They both started screaming at me, then she began to argue with my husband, saying I was not expected til Saturday. In their tempest, they failed to see me record the event on my cell phone. She starting berating him for being so reckless and stupid. Then he threatened me again, saying I had no business being there, telling me if I did not leave they would use more force to get me out of the house. As he said this, he grabbed my arm, threw me to the ground, and slapped and kicked me. I then noticed lines of cocaine on one of the tables, and restraints and whips in the room. My God, I never expected this. Then, out of fear, I grabbed my clothes and ran to my car, then drove to the police station to file domestic abuse charges and get a restraining order against him.

"The police went back to the house with a search warrant and restraining order. When they arrived to arrest him and search the house, they found them both in bed, snorting cocaine, with his girlfriend in handcuffs restrained to the bed. They were both arrested. I took the cell phone recording along with the restraining order, search warrant, and the pictures taken of me at the local emergency room showing the bruises he inflicted on me, to a local attorney to draw up my divorce papers. The attorney had my husband served while he was in jail awaiting trial because he had failed to secure a bond. The attorney looked into the ownership of the property to discover the name on the deed was Saint Thomas University. My husband was meeting up with this woman at the house every month, when he told me he was going in for his rehab. My attorney then turned the story over to the local news station. It turned into a media event. Since I was not the owner of the house, I was not allowed to stay there. Now free of him, finally, I headed back to Dutchess to avoid the media circus. So I called you, to give me moral support."

"Wow, Candy, quite the story. It does bring this train wreck into focus. What are your plans now Candy?"

"Well, Roland, I do not want to sound forward or to be a woman of compromised morals. I am all alone, I have no one I can turn to or trust. It will take time to settle my affairs so I have limited funds. My parents are not aging well, and in declining health, and to place this burden on them a second time would be fatal. I could not do this to them again. I understand you have a roomy artist's loft. Please do not misjudge my intentions, can I stay at your place to hide and lick my wounds for a while. I am feeling very vulnerable, betrayed, not to mention feeling played like a fool. I need time to think, and to get myself established. Please – help me Roland, I have no one to turn to."

I was quite moved by her story, and understood what was going on at the university. And how they had made a scapegoat out of me.

"Candy, your words are as earnest as they are painful. You can stay at my place, there is plenty of room, and much there to keep you occupied, my library, art studio, guitars, cameras, not to mention I am a good cook."

As she turned to me I saw that childlike smile break that mask of her pain. I still can feel that warm Kundalini energy run through my body like a raging river. We then just looked at each other and laughed. Amor fati!

She was no longer that naive farm girl from Idaho; rather, she was now a mature woman of 30, battle tested by life by no choice of her own. She had been made a fool and violated by the guise of false love. Now she felt betrayed, used, and mocked by inferiors.

Although we were separated by twenty-plus years of life, we found common ground in our emotional intelligence, grit, and an alienation from a corrupt world that survives on making victims of the just. We also shared an obsession to know the "why" behind one's actions, and the fortitude to be dauntless in our battles of life.

We spent the rest of the day just being lazy without any plans. We just sat at our table sipping espresso coffee, watching old man river age in peace. On the drive back to my place we stopped at a few roadside farms. I was ad-libbing the day, was not sure where it was going. Where were we going? What we were expecting from each other?

"O, Candy, how about picking out a few things at the farm, and I will create something to make for dinner? Do you have any favorite dishes?"

"Nothing in particular, surprise me, Roland!"

As I picked through the vegetables, I inquired, "Candy, I forgot to ask, are you a vegetarian?"

"Only when I am eating my vegetables Roland. Remember, I was raised on a farm."

"Well, Candy, this is my home; as you can see it's an artist's loft, open living at its best. Just find a place to hunker down."

"Roland, it is very bohemian – it's all you, for sure."

With an equal amount of trepidation and curiosity, she ventured to explore my empire of limited radius. First walking around the living area, then to my library, and art gallery, as she navigated past my myriad guitars.

"Well, Candy, you must be a bit tired from your flight, and week of trials and tribulations. Your timing is impeccable; I spent the weekend cleaning up the house. So you can take my bedroom up in the loft, it has its own private bathroom. And, I will sleep on the couch or the floor. So feel free to settle in and get comfortable. To be forewarned, the interior design was done by a good avant-garde architect friend of mine, designed for a bachelor lifestyle. As you can see, the shower is open, and set under the skylight, the walls are made of Italian marble and designed with multiple spray jets – cleanliness is next to Godliness, and besides it is easy to operate, and clean. So when you decide to shower, let me know, I can go into town to allow you your privacy."

"Thank you, Roland, I appreciate your chivalry, it is reminiscent of the good old days growing up in Idaho – it seems lost in our modern world. Roland … wouldn't you agree, Roland?"

"Totally, Candy."

"Well, Roland, I will need to shower and change into something casual, just give me a half hour or so. Then I will start to wash and cut the vegetables, and set the table while you are gone. What are you planning for dinner?"

"Ummmmh, farro pasta with peas, pancetta, and herbs … one of my favorites; the recipes are in the notebook on the table. Will you need more time, Candy?"

"Not necessary – I was raised in a house with one bathroom with four siblings. This is a cake walk."

When I returned with some items and a bottle of wine, I was not sure if she drank, or would take it as an innuendo of poor social graces on my part. When I arrived home, she was dressed in jeans and a sweatshirt, unpacked and settled in. She had cut and cleaned the vegetables. As I began to prepare the dinner, I asked if she would like something to drink, water, juice or wine. She opted for a glass of wine, preferably a red from one of the local wineries. She was very articulate, well versed, and had an appreciation for the local vintners. Fortunately for me, I also bought local, and had a well-stocked wine closet, thanks to my good friend and wine expert – Rebecca – a frequent guest, and sometimes nemesis. We sat in the living area sipping wine, as I allowed Candy the time to continue on with her story, and her new life plans now being divorced, and on her own for the first time. We had a quiet dinner, along with great conversation, she had an inquisitive mind and was also a great conversationalist. She was very astute in her social graces. After an hour or so of sharing her stories. She interjected, by turning the conversation in my direction.

"Why, Roland, I never knew you were also an artist and musician, you never shared these talents with your students. We all thought highly of you as a professor, enjoyed your quick wit and humor – and how you actually made the dismal science so interesting and relevant. We always were curious as to why such an outgoing person was so guarded with his personal life."

"Well, Candy, thank you for the nice comments. Regarding the art, I enjoy black and white photography, sketching in ink, painting, writing, and of course playing the blues. I play out often at a cool artists' café, Demitasse, in Poughkeepsie."

"Roland, then you must take me there this weekend. Promise me."

"I promise! For not many young folks appreciate the blues –

it will be a lost music form in a generation or two."

"Well, Roland, you will keep it alive with me. Roland, pardon my candor, now that I have seen you in a new perspective, free of the restraints of the classroom, I am sensing you are a person of deep spiritual awareness ... as you would always say ... a statistical outlier. You are equally misunderstood, and underappreciated for your intellectual mind. And I sense you're hiding your enlightened soul out of fear of being condemned for the crime of being too large for your own mortality. You are a mystery that offers answers to those who seek wisdom, though no one listens or comprehends you.

"Roland, you don't have to be your self-effacing humble self with me. I am not out to stone you like the others. While you were out I took the liberty to peek into your library and meditation room – Please, Roland, I will not scorn you. Is it true you are a practicing Magnus/Mystic? I took the liberty to read your meditations, Roland – this is not another witch hunt. I am moved, and also ashamed of denying my soul of the food it seeks. I understand, Roland, speak to me about life and the soul, like you lecture about so freely and discourse about in social economics, and ethics.

"Roland, you helped me remove the mask of my childhood, to reveal my strengths of maturity and true womanhood. Please, share your story with me. I feel I was drawn to you for a purpose I am unable to comprehend. I want to learn about my soul, not to condemn yours."

"Candy, your words are earnest and heartfelt, with true intentions and convictions. I doubt you not, Candy. I have elected to take the arduous path of this life. My world is not understood nor appreciated, and nonetheless accepted by the profane. How can one bring light to a world that walks in the dark with blindfolds?"

"Roland, I did not pry – you left a lot of your writings and meditations on your library table. I thought all the graphs and charts were your artwork. I only went to take a closer look to better view your artwork. I did not realize it was your ritual talismans, and gnostic Christian writing to seek light. Roland! You are a practitioner of the elevated grades of esoteric Freemasonry, and member of the Illuminati?"

"Candy, we carry no titles for our seeking souls, only the labels the profane place upon us unjustly. Do you now also look at me as the outlier to be feared, for bringing hope and light into a humanity in distress?"

"Roland, no! Never! Roland! My new discovery has only heightened my appreciation of you. Roland, I need the strength to survive and to carve a destiny for myself. How, Roland?"

"Candy, look at me, remove those tears from your eyes, smile, take a deep breath, and inhale this moment. Now, exhale this memory to be shared with the heavens. *Amor fati*. Candy, one's fate is their destiny. Our yesterdays are the foreign land from whence we came. The future does not exist until it arrives. We cannot walk back into the past that no longer exists any easier than we can walk into a future that does not exist. Our eternity is in the moment, and in this moment we can cleanse our sins of the past, and accept the future if and when it arrives."

As Candy exhaled, she smiled, and sighed in peace. She gazed into my face. "Thank you, Roland, I am now beginning to understand your world of the Mystic."

"Candy, I am a bit of a night owl. There is a nice cafe up the street, it's open all night, and they showcase some rather good acoustic performers. They have a good crowd. Want to check it out?"

"For sure, Roland, but I have to ask, do you ever sleep or slow down?"

"I am afraid I can't; it's the mystic's curse, for once we stop, we die, and we are not permitted to die until we finish our earthly work. I still have a lot of the 'Great Work' to complete."

"O, Roland, just what in heaven's name are you talking about now? You are going to have to explain this to me also!"

We were now feeling comfortable with ourselves, as we sipped our coffee watching some rather good local talents into the early hours of the morning.

"Well, Roland, it's 2:30 in the morning. I am feeling a little tired from the jet lag."

"I am sorry Candy, I forget, sometimes I get so involved with life, I fail to realize I am a part of it. I always feel like I am an innocent bystander, just watching life, like it is a movie without a plot."

"O you Mystics! Let's head back, the walk back should be magical under this harvest moon ... reminds me of my childhood days in Idaho growing up on the farm."

She took my hand and held it tight. I felt her energy in me, as I watched her facial aura light up. She was born with that inner light in her soul, and cast it into my seeking soul – It meandered through my body like a powerful river. She had awakened my Kundalini serpent power that had been dormant for so long. She then placed her arm around me to give me a kiss. We stopped for a moment to embrace and kiss passionately, then continued on our way back to the loft, viewing all the quaint closed shops in Beacon.

"O, Roland, this has truly been such a magical evening. Did you cast a spell on me, Roland, with your magic?"

"O, Candy, you give me far too much credit. I believe you cast your magic charm on me."

As we entered my loft, she was smiling and radiant. We sat for a while sipping some wine.

"So, Roland, what's on your agenda for tomorrow? A busy schedule, no doubt."

"Not so bad, I have an early morning macro class, a few errands to run, visit a client. I should be back early afternoon. I can let you have use of one of the cars if you have errands to do, or if you are bored."

"Bored in your studio – never. I can just spend eternity in your huge gallery, or take advantage of listening to your music collection. Well, I will check out some of your blues recordings, just to bring myself up to speed for our Saturday evening date at Demitasse. Why, Roland, who are some of your favorite bluesmen? I can check them out while you're out."

"O, I kind of like them all, John Lee Hooker, Muddy Waters, B.B. King, Howling Wolf; these recordings should get you to understand and appreciate the blues."

"Thanks Roland, I will check them out. And thanks for the use of your car, I just need to take care of a few minor legal things. Hey, what is the dress attire for Demitasse? I want to dress right, maybe pick up a new outfit or two for the evening."

"It's casual and laid back … a real artist vibe."

"Well, I am going to catch up on some sleep. What time are you getting up, and showering, you know, with the open shower arrangement, and thanks again for letting me have one of the bathrooms for myself to place my things, and a special thanks for one of the closets too."

"Well, I have to be up early, and out of the house by 8-ish."

"Roland, I will be fast asleep."

"Well, good night Roland, sweet dreams, and I will make dinner for us tonight, it will be a surprise."

I woke up the following morning around 7. Candy was sleeping, I heard no stirrings from the bedroom loft. I jumped into the open shower, dressed and headed out. The day was rather uneventful – how exciting can macroeconomics be? Went to the studio for my weekly radio broadcast, typical daily routines, a few on-the-run client meetings, then headed back home around dinner time. When I arrived, the table was set, with candles lit, and some meditative music playing. Candy was in the kitchen preparing dinner. I thought to myself, I could never recall such tranquil moments with any other woman in my life. Then lamented, only to be young again … what if?

She brought over the serving dishes, then graciously served the plates. She already had the wine decanted, with crystal glasses waiting to be filled. She made an impressive seafood paella. I returned her gracious gestures with a sincere compliment. She returned it with equal grace. We started our dinner conversation with small talk. I can remember with pleasure our conversations, and her impeccable table etiquette.

"So, Roland, I should have asked upon arriving, are you seeing someone now? I hope I am not causing any problems being here?"

"Nothing to concern yourself with right now. I am playing it rather cautious with the dating scene, with my divorce finalized after spending thirty years in a poorly matched marriage. I am just playing the field. Met some rather nice women, shared some rather memorable romantic interludes. But, as of now, not committed."

"So, Roland, please, you need not be so guarded, I am no longer your student. Remember I am a woman who just escaped a very hostile marriage. I shared some of these painful stories with you. So what was the reason for your divorce, and how old are your children? I am sure I can learn something from your experience; was it painful for you as well – Roland? Were there any similarities, and any lessons learned? You can share with me."

"True, Candy, it is important to share such information with another confidant, it either validates or condemns our actions."

"Roland, I do not believe you are capable of uncommendable behavior. Please go on."

"Candy, we just were not right for each other, we lived in different worlds. I speak without vanity, nor malice, nor sense of being uppity or too high-brow. She is very blue collar, and as you know, I am not. I say this with no derision. I come from a learned and humble background. But I have a passion to learn, to challenge myself, and was blessed with my father's artistic blood and my mother's intellect – she was a banker. I wanted to live the examined life, and live life to the fullest. It became rather evident, early on in the marriage, it was not working for us.

"She was a good woman, and like all of us had to fight her demons, some just do it better than others. I found myself attending faculty parties all alone, the business dinners alone, the opening days at the galleries alone, and the champagne dinners that followed alone. She never supported me when I played out with a blues band, and on it went. I had exhausted myself in trying to make her at least be a little part of my world. She was not a romantic, very inhibited, not at all sensual. I was always alone, had no one to share my joys or pains with. For she simply viewed life as a series of endless errands and obligations, and her entertainment was simply watching T.V. – Why, she never even inquired about what degrees I held, what courses I taught, what kind of consulting I did. She didn't know where my studio was located – she just never cared, was never interested. To make matters worse, her family had a disdain for me, and did not trust educated white-collar professionals. Even on the holidays I found myself alone – she would take our two girls over to her family's house, so they would not be contaminated by my educated family.

"To be celibate and lonely by choice is a sin, especially when one does not have to. I never cheated on her … But I always had thoughts of doing so, for I knew I needed real female companionship. I stayed in the marriage for the sake of honor, and my daughters. But the cost became too expensive for me to afford emotionally. Then, one day a mutual friend informed me she was having an affair with an old friend from her childhood neighborhood."

"Roland, you must have been devastated."

"Actually, I saw it as a blessing; I am not an emotional person. It was the perfect escape. What hurt was the fact that my daughters knew about this, and helped cover her tracks. The man she fell for was the one she should have married in the first place. He was a dropout, spent a few years in the service, a person with no direction. Well, she just jumped on the Harley, for her bar hopping was more to her liking than gallery hopping, and the good life. She could never appreciate the importance of the esthetics of life. They are happy now. There were no arguments. I only wished that she would have shared her intentions with me sooner, so I could have started to make plans for myself."

"Roland, your morality precedes you. Since the divorce have you been intimate with a woman?"

"O, Candy, I profess to be no saint, only a good man attempting to do what is right, and to find a true good woman. O heavens, yes, I have been blessed to find the company of a few good women with like interests. Excuse my candor, I have a lot of life to catch up on."

"O, Roland, now I understand why you are always on the move, always doing something new, achieving new goals, while setting more goals on your horizon. You are an interesting man who has accomplished a lot, and who enjoys sharing it with your friends. Though I believe your mysteries conceal far more than what you reveal."

"Ha, Candy, you know, you never get in trouble for the things you don't say."

"True, Roland, though you will never forgive yourself for those words you failed to share out of fear, and for the sake of diplomacy."

"Well-said, Candy – soon a change in heart will reveal a new mystery or two?"

She just stared at me with those beautiful blue eyes. Then held up her glass of wine, "Roland, a toast to unraveling life's mysteries, and to Saturday night; we will both free ourselves from the emotional chains of our broken marriages – and past. Will the Magnus exorcise those demons that thwart our search for happiness? What is this Light you talk of Roland? Harbor it not within you – cast it for the sake of your soul ... and mine."

We talked until dawn, having lost track of time as we laughed, sipped wine, and reminisced about some of my past lectures, philosophy, art, music. It was the first time in my life I felt so much happiness, inside of myself and externally. It was cathartic, I once believed this only happens in fiction. For the first time since she arrived I thought to myself, how far I can take this? I was enjoying Candy far too much to believe she was just a true friend, and now wanted to breach her soul as my lover.

"Roland, it is dawn, we have been talking all night, and you have to work today."

"No problem, Candy, I have time. Besides, I don't need much sleep. Just jump into the shower and dress while I prepare the coffee and a quick breakfast for us."

"No problem, Roland, after breakfast I will just tidy up the loft after you leave to teach, then crash on the couch to catch a few Z's."

"Fine, Candy, I will catch up with you later in the day."

"Fine, Roland. What are our plans for tonight?"

"I will think of something, since you were gracious enough to make dinner last night.

"Well, Roland, while you're in the kitchen, I am going to jump into the shower for a few minutes."

Being a gentleman I tarried in the kitchen until I heard the shower stop running, knowing it was OK to head out of the kitchen – one of the few rooms that had walls – I had some eccentric taste in design, and looked to push the limits of convention. When the shower water was silenced, I waited a few more minutes so as not to impose on her modesty. As I left the kitchen, Candy was still drying herself off in the shower. She then wrapped the towel around her body then returned to have breakfast together.

"Well, I am going to jump into the shower then dress for class."

"No problem Roland … I won't peek."

"After class, I am going to head to Poughkeepsie to pick up some photography and art supplies, then while in the area, I have to stop at the lab for my routine blood work. I should be back around 5-ish."

"Don't rush, Roland, I am just going to hunker down for the day … your lifestyle is exhausting … maybe do some reading, and listen to some music from your collection. I plan to check out that John Lee Hooker guy. Hey, Roland, why the blood test, you alright?"

"You will really like John Lee Hooker, and don't worry, my health is fine – today."

When I arrived home, I found her asleep on the couch, wearing only one of my button-down shirts, with a blanket somewhat wrapped about her. I did not want to disturb her. I went to my library to drop off a few books I just purchased, and noticed a few of my sacred books on the library table flipped over. It looked like Candy did some reading during the day, I walked over to the books, and was quite surprised to see the books she found of interest, the *Kama Sutra, Tantric Love Making* and *Sexual Alchemy*. I left them in place, and read the pages she had marked with paper clips. I walked out of the library and gently closed the door, then went to my gallery to do some pen and ink sketches for my next gallery opening. A few moments later I heard her get up as she entered the gallery.

"Sorry Roland, I must have dosed off for a while, I had to catch up on my sleep. What are you working on, you sketch some interesting subjects – do you know them personally?"

"Just some friends, for some odd reason I have placed all of my subjects behind castles, and medieval settings. I like to keep sketches of all my friends for old times' sake."

"Well, I hope I am a worthy of friendship Roland, will you sketch me?" "With pleasure, my lady Candice, just move closer to the light coming from the window, so I can capture you in all your perfection."

"Roland, will you exhibit my portrait at your gallery opening?"

"Candy, I will be honored to have you as part of my exhibit."

"So, Roland, what will you name this work of yours?"

"Ummh … I am not sure … for some unknown reason, I am thinking, *The Bride of the Languedoc.*"

"Roland, why this title?"

"Candy, I am not sure, it was as if someone just whispered it into my head."

"Roland, are the hierarchies talking to you again?"

"Candy, how do you know about the hierarchies?"

"Roland, you left your occult rituals and meditations pinned to the wall."

"Candy, will you persecute me as a heretic too?"

"Roland, Heavens no! I had a beautiful dream on the first night I slept at your loft. I was full of light, then a voice whispered to me, 'Follow the Light – for it will be extinguished soon.' What does this mean Roland? Please tell me, who are you? What are you hiding from me? You can see the future? Now, damn it, talk to me Roland!"

"O, Candy, I have always been honest with you; I am a man of transparency. It is only the profane who fail to see and comprehend the truth out of fear. For them the truths are seen as darkness, giving them license to persecute the just. You know the frailty of the human spirit. When given a choice between the light and darkness the crowds will always clamor and shout out … *Give us Barabbas.*

"Candice, I love you, but not just for the flesh, but from the depths of my heart and soul. For if it was not for your heart and soul, I would not be able to give you a second look. For if this were not true, I would still be entertaining Nancy's folly. As for the future, it does not exist, for it has not arrived. When it does arrive it is no longer the future but the present, then in a mere few hours it is the past, a land of exile to which we cannot return.

"Candy, remember: as above, so below … as below, so above. It is the spiritual axiom for all true seekers of the Light. Harmony can only be achieved by the analogy of opposites."

"Roland, please tell me, is this why destiny has brought us together? Roland, I am confused as ever now. What are you saying? What are you trying to tell me? What is it that I should know?"

"Candy, like the lost troubadours of the Occitan, I believe it best to sing my story from my heart and soul. For we will now free ourselves from the profane, and rise above they who only know the language of the flesh, who reduce their communications to flattery and lies. My Lady Candice, please allow me to sing my poem to you, accompanied by my lute. For read not the words, but the truth that is found between the lines. I dedicate my October song to your loving soul."

The October Tree

An angel whispered my name today
Disguising herself as a premature October breeze
To cool my burning summer thoughts
She guided me to a magical oak tree
Rooted deep within my soul

She guided me to
The land of whence she came
And, was given a new name
One I have never known
She admonished me to abandon my life of old
My heart now glistened like gold

Forget not your new name
And, your remaining days well
Be not a profane fool
Who believes you can tame God's fools

The language of the heavens is not parchment bound
Its tongue is inscribed in the heavens above
And, those seeking souls in the earth below

Heaven's language is eternal and true
With a memory of every word spoken
Unlike the tongue of man
With words that fade
Like footprints in the snow

For if you seek heaven's crown
Look yonder upon heaven's tree
Now grown tall and wide
Now rooted deep
Within your wounded soul

Heaven has heard your fiery cries
That have risen like smoke
From your once burning eyes
Blessing you with shade
With October's cool days
Release your sorrows
For heaven is finally in your tomorrows

Heaven has planted your destiny at birth
By having you grow into a celestial oak
Surviving life's storms and assaults
You marked your victories long
With your sad songs

Your fruits you now bear
Are ripe and sweet
Only for the palettes of seeking souls
Though bitter to the bite of the profane
For soon you will be freed from the earth's reigns

Child of time be warned
Better to be a lone oak planted on a hill
Than to be counted as a grain of sand
In the vast desert of humanity

Now armed with wisdom
And a child's heart
Your tree marks high
For soon you will depart

Your October tree will bloom
With leaves of crimson and gold
Then fall
One by one
To earth's fertile ground below

Fear not the autumn of your life
For your tree is now within heaven's site
Climb it high to heaven's door
To be welcomed with light
And never more to be scorned
By the profane below.

Now my Candice dear
Hear my serenade
That sings like the nightingale of old
Perched high upon heaven's tree
To awaken you from your mortal sleep
We now have a calling to fulfill
Tarry not ... for heaven can't wait

With Love
Roland

Candy's eyes brimmed with tears. "Roland? I am not sure how I should respond, your words are beautiful. Should I be happy for you, or should I mourn your song? Roland, tell me what is going on!"

"Candy, please, not now, we have a beautiful life planned together, we are destined for great things."

"O, Roland, you are too much of an enigma for me!"

"O, Candy, now this is the kindest compliment you can give a mystic! Now let us not tarry on our destiny's path! Amor fati!

"Well, Roland, on that note, I really enjoyed those blues recordings of yours. I hope for old times' sake you will also play me one of your blues tunes."

"I promise, Saturday night at Demitasse. It will be an evening of memories for eternities to come."

"Well, Candy, do you like Italian food?"

"Who doesn't? Why?"

"There is a great little Italian restaurant just within walking distance, small, quiet, very intimate. I will call to make reservations, say, for 8."

"OK, Roland, while you make the call I will jump into the shower. Roland, I must say you have quite an eclectic library. Do you have a favorite subject, or books you hold dear or stimulating? What are all those books on Gnosticism, and ritual meditations, and sexual alchemy? I am a country girl who has never been exposed to the Adepts of Europe as you have. Will you share this knowledge with me? Show me the Light?"

"Candy, it is not for the faint of heart, only for an earnest soul seeking the arduous path."

"Roland, I can handle it, what does it take?"

"An open mind, resolve, the desire to find transcendence, and fear not to rise above the profane."

"Roland, I did not intend to snoop or invade your privacy.

You left a few of your spiritual notebooks out again with your meditations on Christian occultism, and Kabala, a true Adept you are, no doubt. Well, Roland, it looks like we are going to have a rather busy weekend together."

"Let's tarry not. While you make reservations, I will shower and dress. I should be ready in no time."

We were becoming very comfortable with each other by now, and less inhibited over the days. When I walked out of the kitchen, Candy was toweling herself off in the open shower area. She seemed to be comfortable with her nudity. She looked up and asked, "I assume the dress code is casual."

"Just throw on a pair of jeans and a sweater and you will fit right in."

"OK, Roland, I brought down a few towels for you so you can take a quick shower before we head up. I am heading upstairs to dress."

She was beautiful, as she once again walked up the stairs, exposing her beautiful naked skin and form. What man could forsake such a woman? I jumped in the shower. As I was dressing, Candy came downstairs to announce she was ready for dinner, and on time.

I reserved my favorite table for two at the front corner of the restaurant by the window offering a beautiful October streetscape. We ordered a bottle of Chianti, made a toast to our budding friendship. She then started to open up to talk about her recent divorce.

"Roland, you only met my husband once, the night you escorted me home. You saw him for what he is – a monster. He beat me, cheated on me, and always put me down in public. At all his business gatherings and parties he always ignored me, and would run to every woman that struck his fancy. He would not talk to me all evening, or introduce to me his lady friends."

"This should have raised a few flags, Candy."

"Well, I also found some photos of him and that whore together at a party. He is a sick man; at the last party we attended together, true to his MO, he left me as soon as we entered the party to go flirt with all the women. Then, an innocent bystander who was observing his behavior came over to talk to me, a real gentleman, and tried to make me feel better, and he brought me a drink. He was a married man, of well-known good character. He started talking about his wife and children – believe me – no man uses a wife and children as a pickup line. He was just trying to help.

"When my husband saw me talking to him, he ran across the room and grabbed my arm, and berated me, calling me a whore in front of everyone. When this man interceded on my behalf, telling him this is no way to treat a woman – let alone your wife, he became very belligerent and out of control. He pushed the man down, then started to kick him. He had to be restrained. I left him at the party; he did not return home till dawn.

"When he arrived home high and disheveled, he starting yelling at me for hitting on all those men, and for the first time hit me. When he sobered up he did not remember anything that happened. What do you think, Roland?"

"He has some serious issues: anger, drinking, drugs, sex addictions. Sounds like DID – Dissociative Identity Disorder."

"Roland, what the hell is that?"

"Multiple personalities."

"Roland, have you ever known anyone like this?"

"Regretfully – a few."

"Candy, how did a sweet, beautiful and intelligent woman like you fall for a guy like that?"

"We met back in Idaho. We went to high school together, and he also attended the same Methodist church as my family. He was good looking, very smart, we even dated a few times in high school, and he was always a gentleman. Then he left for college at a prestigious university, was awarded a full scholarship, graduated top of his class. A large computer behemoth recruited him on the condition he complete a master's in physics, to be paid by the company. The company was generous, they allowed him to attend full time, with a sizeable living stipend. When he completed it, he was hired as an executive in their fast-track program. The company had a major manufacturing and research facility near our hometown.

"He returned as the conquering hero, and favorite son. We then reconnected, and started dating, then were engaged. At the time it was so normal, he was a pure gentleman, a deacon in the local church, well loved by everyone. I dated him for months before I allowed him to kiss me. He moved up the corporate ladder very fast, and before long he was offered a senior management position at their corporate headquarters here in Dutchess County. We immediately made plans to marry in our home community before we moved east. It seemed nothing could stop us; we were living the American dream. We purchased a house, furnished it and were living the good life. Though something was missing, or amiss.

"Once we moved east he began to change. We spent less and less time together, and to cure my boredom and loneliness I enrolled as an adult student in the business program at Saint Thomas University. But the home front was deteriorating, he stopped coming home for dinner, not even calling to inform me. He was not affectionate or romantic. I began to doubt myself, believing it was my fault. Thinking I must be a plain-Jane country girl, boring and unsophisticated by East Coast standards. He was the first man I was intimate with, and it was consummated on our wedding night. He also said I was the first woman he was intimate with.

"It was only after a few months of moving here, we stopped having sex. He never seemed interested. I really believed it was me, being the good, old-fashioned girl. So one day, I went shopping for the sexiest lingerie, had my hair done, and bought some champagne. When he did eventually return home, I hoped I would surprise him. We went to bed, then he just fell asleep, not even taking notice of me. I was feeling lost and alone with no real friends to talk to."

"After he was arrested and the police searched the house, I was shocked to learn the double life he was leading right in front of my face. They found cocaine, ecstasy, pornography, and he was having sex orgies that included S&M, bondage. I understand as part of his sentence he had to attend a rehabilitation center for his drug and sex addictions. He was also having a number of affairs with married women. It is on the police blotter that he was threatened by a number of very unhappy husbands."

"Roland, should I have picked up on this when I started dating him? Was it my insecurity?"

"You were young, and may not have known, or were too humble to see yourself as the beautiful woman you truly are. I intend not a word of flattery, just a genuine and sincere compliment. You made the right decision to leave him, and not a moment too soon, and for all the right reasons."

"Looking back, Roland, I don't know why I stayed so long. His behavior and how he treated me was outright disrespectful."

"What else did he do that hurt you? It was not just the physical infidelity, it was the emotional infidelity as well."

"Such as?"

"He would mock me at parties in front of his friends at social events. He would attend parties behind my back attended by mutual friends, telling them to say nothing to me. Then these same people would stare me in the face, lying with a straight face, making a fool out of me, telling me what a good marriage we have."

"Roland, what kind of person does this sort of thing? Have you ever encountered this?"

"Candy, he does not consider you or your relationship when he behaves this way. He is selfish and acts on what makes him feel good. You are not part of the equation when alcoholism and substance abuse feed his addictions and violence. Candy, you are wise to have left him. There would be nothing to gain by staying with him, since he will only be happy when you are sad and miserable. And, you are right, when people see how poorly he treats you, you will also lose their respect as well. They will doubt your self-worth, see you as too naïve, weak, believing you lack confidence, and incapable of making a good decision. Candy, you are far too beautiful, intelligent, moral, and classy to be involved with an office whore."

"Roland, you speak with conviction or experience, have you ever experienced this?"

"Many a good person shares your story. Such people are merely skin-tags that need to be cut off, otherwise they grow and make you look ugly."

"Roland, maybe there is something about this synchronicity you often speak of?" Do you believe this is what brought us together? And, for what purpose? Or did you cast one of your magical rituals on me?"

"Candice, an Adept of White Magic, is a true seeker of Light, and is obligated to use the laws of alchemy to transmute their own souls. Tampering with another person's soul for personal gain violates and encroaches on the Almighty's plan for such a person. To violate this sacred law is to walk on the dark side.

Amor fati, one must follow the plans of heaven. For our fate is our destiny. We have been brought together for a reason that we will not live to see – for synchronicity is blind for those who possess its sight. Your husband was a dark abyss, when you cast your light and love into his dark, demon-infested soul, he saw the light, but comprehended it not. Never throw pearls before swine."

Back at the loft, she put on some soft meditative music, lit some candles she had purchased. She moved close to me, and we caressed, falling asleep on the couch. We found ourselves still in our evening's caress when we awoke. Candy got up and went to shower, I soon joined her.

"Roland, I am finally getting to understand your design concepts for this open, barrier-free living. It is rather liberating."

"I take it you are not an inhibited person? The finest tailored clothing made of the most exotic fabrics can never dress an ugly soul."

She turned to me and we began to hug, kiss, and caress under the streams of warm water that covered our nudity.

"Roland, let's wait till tonight after our date at Demitasse, I want to make this special for us. And, you have an early morning Saturday class. I will need to borrow one of the cars to do some shopping for an outfit for this evening. What do you baby boomer blues guys like – maybe something nostalgic, or redux?"

"O, Candy, surprise me. I am sure you will look great in anything you wear."

"I am thinking avant-garde bohemian, or some kind of hippie chic?"

Wrestling with Heaven
(Roland's Dream Journal)

"Caedite eos. Novit enim Dominus qui sunt eius"
("Kill them all, the Lord will recognize His own.")
- Arnaud-Amaury
Papal Legate 1209

I was again woken by my nightmare, though this time I was calm, and a sense of peace descended upon me. As my Holy Guardian Angel appeared to me at the end of my "dream," commanding me to recite the following prayer in order to recall and record this vision, and to meditate on it daily while fasting.

Come forth on to me, Thou that art my true self: my Light: my Soul come forth unto me: Thou that art crowned with Glory: That art the Changeless: The unnameable: The Immortal Godhead, whose Place is in the Unknown: and whose Dwelling is the Abode of the Undying Gods. Heart of my soul; self-shining Flame, Glory of Light, Thee I invoke. Come forth unto me, my Lord: to me: who am Thy reflection in the mighty sea of Matter! Hear Thou Angel and Lord! Hear Thou in the habitations of Eternity; come forth; and purify to Thy Glory My Mind and Will! Without Thee am I nothing; in Thee am I All-self- existing in Thy Selfhood to eternity!

As I fell back into the reverie of recalling my dream, as my eyes closed and I fell into a trance-like state I experienced this vision: I was standing on the parapet of a castle in the company of many knights and men of arms prepared for battle. There were many holy men and women in the streets below that looked like monks taking the women and children to a safe sanctuary as they prayed, and gave them blessings. These monks were revered by the knights and men of arms, who referred to these holy beings as the Prefecti of the Cathar faith. One of the Prefecti, an old bearded man, was carrying what appeared to be many holy books and a treasure, to be taken to a safe refuge. The Prefecti, many of whom were women, went about laying their hands upon the women and men that did not take up arms, and the children offering them their final Consolamentum, the Cathar's only sacrament that is administered at death to remove all our sins, and to induct us into the spiritual degree of the Prefecti, as they walked us to heaven's golden light, now free of our mortal dross. The knights kept a grim vigil on the horizon. It was a beautiful summer day in the Languedoc, July 22, 1209 – The Feast day of Saint Mary Magdalene. A holy day for both Catholics, and the "heretic" Cathars, living within the walled city of Beziers – home to both Cathars and Catholics. It was also intended to be my wedding day, to Constance of Albi. We were to be wed later in the day, in the fields of the majestic Occitan region, overlooking the city of Beziers, in Cathar fashion with the Bishop, Prefecti, and Credentes, along with friends, and Count Raymond VI of Toulouse – in whose army I now served with fidelity.

Pope Innocent III in his attempt to rid Southern France of all the heretics and their supporters – the Lords of the Trencavel – launched the Albigensian Crusade under the banner of King Philip Augustus of France. The crusade was to be led by the papal legate Arnaud-Amaury, Abbot of Citeaux. King Philip delegated the siege of Beziers to his most ambitious and blood lusting Baron, Simon de Montfort.

On the horizon we saw the crusaders' pavilions, and the banners of the King planted in the fields before us. There were also the Knights Templar in the vanguard of the approaching army. Simon de Montfort sent his messengers along with the Abbot, under a flag of truce to the closed city gate, to offer the terms of surrender, and to spare the city of its destruction. The Abbot was accompanied by a few crusaders, and the Grand Master of the Templars. The Abbot presented the local Catholic bishop and me their terms: Release all the heretic "Christian" Cathars within your city walls to the church for execution or conversion; have the excommunicated Count Raymond denounce his support for the Cathars and turn his support to the church in this crusade for their extermination. They were to return in an hour for my decision. I signed the Grand Master of the Templars in due and ancient form, our oath of fidelity. He returned the oath, unbeknownst to the Abbot, then in defiance of the pope, he exited the field of battle with his Templars, leaving the devil's work of human butchery to the Abbot and crusaders. I looked down to the crowded streets below. I saw Constance in her wedding gown, kneeling on the ground receiving her final Consolamentum. As the Abbot returned with his crusader's color guard, Bethany, one of the young Prefecti, approached me to give me my Consolamentum.

The Abbot then approached the wall on horseback with his retinue demanding our answer. The Catholic bishop and I consulted, before we gave our formal response.

"I, Roland of Beziers, speak in the name of my earthly lord, Count Raymond VI of Toulouse, and the rightful sovereign Lord of the Languedoc, The Cathars, and God Almighty ... we will fight to the death for our faith and the sovereignty of the Occitan people, allowing all to practice their faith without fear and persecution. I, Bishop of Beziers, in conformance with my Catholic faith of peace, will not turn over fellow Christians to you to be murdered by a power-hungry church and land-seeking king. In the name of Our Almighty God!"

"I, Arnaud-Amaury, Papal legate, representing his Imminence the most holy Pope Innocent and the French King Philip, hereby acknowledge your response from your rebellious and heretic city ruled by men no better than animal dung, men possessed by the powers of women's menstrual blood."

His bannered retinue laughed and mocked us. In response we released a catapult from behind the city wall laden with animal dung and blood.

Bethany admonished me by reinforcing the fact that as a Cathar I am expected to oppose all violence, obligated to seek death over the killing of another fellow soul.

"And, you must now drop your sword immediately!"

She further informed me that the Cathar Prefecti carrying our Holy Books and sacred treasure was to rendezvous with me and Constance at the church. I was to escape, marry Constance, then take the Holy Books and sacred treasure to Montsegur – the safe mountain – to fulfill the Cathar's mission to build a temple and university of Light. The fulfillment of this mission would bring in the heavenly dispensation to end man's demonic dark world, and to prevent the future coming holocausts of man's self-inflicted destruction.

"Roland, this has been ordained for you, if you fail you will be forced into a series of reincarnations until you satisfy your heavenly mission. Don't let the devil's flesh detract you from your soul's mission. Roland! Now drop your sword, strip yourself of your armor so I can hear your apparellamentum (confession)."

As I dropped my sword, I got down on my knees to accept

my destiny. I offered my confession up to God. Then Bethany began the Consolamentum.

> *Roland Berengiere of Albi, you wish to receive the spiritual baptism by which the Holy Spirit is given in the Church of God, together with the Holy Prayer and the imposition of hands by Good Men. This holy baptism, by which the Holy Spirit is given, the Church of God has preserved from the time of the Apostles until this time, and it passed from Good Men to Good Men until the present moment, and it will continue to do so until the end of the world. Roland keep the commandments of Christ to the upmost of your ability. Do not commit adultery, kill, lie, nor steal. You should turn the other cheek in the face of those who persecute you. Roland Berenguiere of Albi, now to finish your Consolamentum, you must promise to hate this world, and the works and things of this world.*
>
> *Now Roland, before I place my hands upon your head for your acceptance and blessing do you swear to uphold …*

As Bethany was about to finish the Consolamentum, and place her hands on my head a trebuchet was let loose from the crusaders outside the city walls, throwing massive stones over the castle's parapet. I looked on in horror as I saw one of the devil's molten rocks come flying over the parapet, decapitating Bethany as she was preparing to complete my Consolamentum. Her broken body fell to the street below to be trampled by horses, and carts filled with people. Now I was no less the devil as those crusaders now entering the city on their mission of killing and plundering. I picked up my sword to defend Bethany's honor, and to save my wife to be.

The King's army marched into the city with overpowering odds as their siege engines breached our parapets. Soon the crusaders were on the parapets easily picking off all the defenders, then crashed through the main gate. Montfort sent in his ribauds, camp followers that usually served as cannon fodder; they were barefoot beggars armed with only daggers and clubs. Their rewards were usually the remnants of the knight's booty. As the ribauds entered the city they began to strip, rape, and kill women and children. Some of the minority of the Cathars were rounded up. The men, women, and children were stripped naked and then burned at the stake; others were hacked to pieces. The bishop along with many Catholics, and the few remaining Cathars, along with Constance, found refuge in the Church of Mary Magdalene.

Knowing the battle was now lost to the heathens of a satanic god, I fought my way into the church. Here I found the Catholic Bishop serving mass, and Constance along with the last surviving Cathar bishop holding the sacred texts and treasures of our faith. I locked the church door and barricaded its doors and windows as the ribauds approached with the knighted crusaders. We were now all on our knees praying, when the motley army breached the doors. They started to butcher and hack everyone to death, then even pulled the Catholic Bishop from the altar, slit his throat and hacked off his limbs, and stole all the precious jewels and metals from the altar. They killed without mercy, as the crusaders now joined the fray. I fought my way over to Constance, who was now bleeding, and standing over the body of the butchered Catholic bishop and the dead body of our Cathar Bishop, who tucked our sacred books and Treasure under him as he lay dying. Constance, in her bloodied wedding dress, gave me the books and the treasure, telling me the Perfecti ordained me to take our most holy books and treasures, and to secure them in a safe sanctuary in the caves below Montsegur.

"A Templar escort will be waiting for you behind the castle

keep. For you, Roland of Albi, have been ordained to build man's final house of Heaven's Divine Light upon the ruins of Montsegur, with our innocent blood."

I took our Holy Books and our Sacred Treasure from Constance, and gripped her to take her away. A crusader's arrow pierced her heart, she looked up at me bleeding from her mouth then spoke her final words to me.

"Roland our love is now eternally sealed, fear not the pains and injustice of this world … you must now leave my side to save yourself, for the sake of saving humanity from itself."

As I went to give Constance my final embrace and kiss of this world, another crusader fired an arrow into her heart, then a few of the ribauds grabbed her dead body while tearing off her wedding gown, and groped her in their act of necrophilia. I could not believe man had the capability of such hate, and love for genocide. With a few swings of my sword I was able to lop off their miserable fucking ugly heads, then I castrated them throwing their cursed genitals to their fellow swine. I fought my way out of this wretched hell perpetuated by the hands of the Pope. As I found my way out of the city, I saw the flames and putrid smoke rising up from the remains of Mary Magdalene Church. The crusaders rounded up all its inhabitants locked them in churches and burnt them alive, giving no quarter to Catholics or Cathars.

One of the King's barons approached the Pope's prelate, Arnaud-Amaury, inquiring how were they were to tell the heretic Cathars from the Catholics. He responded, *"Caedite eos. Novit enim Dominus qui sunt eius"* – "Kill them all, the Lord will recognize His own."

The crusaders dragged out and slaughtered 20,000 men, women and children. The prisoners were blinded, dragged behind horses, and used for target practice. What remained of the city was razed by fire. Then, the crusaders marched out of the city led by the clerics singing *"Veni Sancte Spiritu."*

After the massacre, Arnaud wrote a letter to Pope Innocent III, "Today your Holiness, twenty thousand heretics were put to the sword, regardless of rank, age or sex. What a blessed day this has been." Satan smiled with delight upon his crusading proxies, knowing the church was now his.

Once outside the city under the cover of darkness, I was approached by mounted Templar knights, who signed the oath of fidelity. One was The Grand Master of the Templars, who pulled my bloodied body onto his horse, placing our Holy Books and Sacred Treasures in a cart. Then he took me with his Vanguard to the caves of Montsegur. We traveled safely in the countryside under his Templar flag.

We found the cave under the mountain fortress of Montsegur, and with the Templar's assistance secured the books and treasures, and marked them for recovery in the near future. They departed, leaving me to tend to the remaining Cathars. Over the following days the remnants of the Cathars filed into the castle of Montsegur, as we worked over the following year to rebuild and reinforce the castle walls, making it our earthly sanctuary. Although a peace treaty was signed between the Pope, the French King, and the Lords of the Trencavel, the Catholic Church continued its persecution of the Cathars. Satan had chained their self-righteous souls to their greedy ambitions.

Over the years I devoted myself to the Cathar faith, was ordained a Cathar Bishop, and continued on with my celibate life, never to look at another woman with passion. My eyes were only for Constance. Besides, why bring another child into this devil's world, where the "Holy" order was the brutal and indiscriminate genocide of innocent men, women, and children.

In June of 1219, the crusaders marched on to Marmande

under Pope Honorius' new Albigensian crusade to continue on with its killings of the innocents. The city's garrison commander realized the city could not hold back the massive crusading army, and sought to negotiate a peaceful surrender of the city. The Bishop of Saintes, along with the William des Roches, accepted the terms. As the city's gates were open to complete the peaceful surrender, the French soldiers entered and began to slaughter all the inhabitants; lords, ladies and their children, women and men. All the inhabitants were stripped naked, slashed and cut to pieces as the army hacked all of the city's inhabitants to death. Like Beziers no quarter was offered. Once again, the "good" soldiers of the All Loving God, found their blessing and rewards with the satanic god of the earth. Next Avignon fell to the crusade, then Montech fell as the garrison at Castelsarrasin was starved into submission. In 1234 the Pope established The Inquisition to uproot the remaining Cathars in the Languedoc and northern Italy. On Friday, May 13, 1239 The Pope's crusading army marched into Mont-Aime in Champagne, where they delivered 183 Cathar men and women to the flames of a waiting bonfire.

Montsegur – meaning safe mountain – the last remaining Cathar stronghold and sanctuary was now targeted by the Pope and King of France for total destruction. It contained the last Cathar convent and seminary, almost impregnable, in a castle sitting atop a rocky crag some 3,500 feet high.

At the end of May 1243, 10,000 crusaders, under the command of Hugh des Arcis, the Seneschal of Carcassonne, along with the Archbishops of Narbonne and Albi, besieged our 400 defenders. In July, in a very clear night sky, the Milky Way revealed many bad omens. Thirty or forty falling stars were observed, a sign that we were now almost ready to return to the spiritual realm whence we came.

After ten long months of holding off the French army, siege engines were erected within striking distance of our walls. Next artillery operations were commenced, throwing massive stones against our walls, which began to crumble under the battering. Realizing we could no longer hold out, many of the remaining knights and Cathars received the Consolamentum. On March 2, 1244, Peter Roger, the Lord of the Castle, surrendered Montsegur to the King of France for his royal control. We were allowed a 15-day reprieve to negotiate the surrender. It was during this period that Mathieu Bonnet, a Believer, Pierre Bonnet, a Prefect, and I, under the cover of darkness, scaled down the steep cliffs of Montsegur with the manuscripts of our Holy Books and the Holy Grail to rendezvous with the Grand Master and a contingent of the Templars. The Grand Master approached me with his sign of fidelity. I then placed our Holy Books, and the Holy Grail into a wagon. The Grand Master then spoke to me.

"Bishop Roland Berengiere of Albi, peace upon you. Your Books and the Holy Grail are now in Holy hands, your work is now complete, and you are free to go home to the land from whence you came. Rest assured, Roland, this treasure is now in safe hands, and will be taken far away across a great ocean to an undiscovered land. It will be held there until a future time when you will return it to this sacred mountain. It will be the new beacon of Divine Light to finally open the eyes of a dark and distressed humanity."

With this we parted ways. I requested he take my two companions with him to a safe sanctuary. I scaled the shear mountain walls, returning to the castle to attend to my flock. During these final days before surrender, I attended to the wounded and sick, offered the knights the conversa, and the Consolamentum to the dying Believers. Under the terms of the surrender, everyone would be spared as long as they submitted themselves to the Inquisition. For Cathars this would require us to renounce our faith, or be burned alive. Out of the remaining castle population of 410, 225 were Cathar Prefecti. As the day of surrender approached, many more Believers and soldiers received the Consolamentum. As we were marched outside the castle gates, the awaiting crusaders stripped the men, women and children, and we were taken to a pyre built at the prat dels cremats ("field of the burned") at the foot of the castle to be burned at the stake. To prolong our suffering, the Inquisition commanded the executioners to use green logs, which take longer to smoke, thus denying us the benefit to die of smoke inhalation before the flames reached us. This was ordered to prolong our suffering and to hear our cries of pain for their entertainment.

As we walked to our death we all cried out our final prayer:

Holy Father, just God of good spirits, who has no falsehood, nor lies, nor errs, nor hesitates for fear of death to sojourn in the world of an alien god, because we are not of the world nor the world us, grant us to know that which You know and love that which You love. The treacherous Pharisees who now hover at the gates of the Kingdom to prevent those who desire to enter from doing so.

I would have rather been crucified than be burned alive. As the flames danced nearer to me, I thought of Constance and Bethany, and the terrible deaths and desecrations they went through. I looked up to the heavens, smiling and feeling blessed, knowing I was now leaving the devil's heaven. The pain of the flames were wicked, as they sizzled and hissed, as my blood fell upon its closing path. I was now bleeding heavily as the flames stripped my skin from my body. I tried to close my eyes so not to see the burning holocaust before me of my fellow Prefect's, men and women, now married in a ring of fire. We were all peaceful. As we smiled and prayed, we no longer felt the flames of death. I was unable to close my eyes from the stinging smoke poking at my eyes, unable to squint or close them because my eyelids had burned off. Next I saw the light of heaven open up before us. We then began to feel heaven's light as our tears of joy extinguished our pains. Then an angel escorted me to a sanctuary upon a high mountain where I saw Constance and Bethany waiting for me with a scroll of instructions to teach me the Enochian language of the Angels.

I spent the rest of the day in contemplation, meditation and cabalistic ritual work. It was at this moment I experienced the divine alchemy transmute my seeking soul. I felt at peace, knowing my life was not in vain. My soul rejoined as I felt heaven's purging fires transmute the dross from my soul into heaven's gold. Now all the trials and tribulations of my life exposed their purpose. I accepted my mission with humble zealotry. Later in the evening I entered the following into my daily meditation journal:

The Siege

O lord, my soul is like that of a besieged citadel sitting high upon a mighty mountain with its ramparts crumbling under the force of a relentless profane enemy that seeks destruction and plunder for the sake of temporal treasures. Deep within the castle's keep of my deep soul, I know my futile stand is just, and not in vain. For I seek not to pillage the treasurers of others. I only seek to preserve the sacred treasures of my seeking soul. A treasure so well guarded that no enemy can conquer it, regardless of how my castle falls.

In my time of desolation and despair, I raise my Godly talisman high – my sacred Rosy Cross of Golgotha – whose scent of its first bloom sweetens the acrid stench of battle.

As the siege of life tramples down my humble ramparts of my mortal life, I find my peace knowing the treasures of God's wisdom and grace await me behind the veil of light.

Since time known, profane mankind has crumbled the castles of the Godly, holding them captive within their own souls. Worthy men will be mocked and persecuted by arrogant and ignorant Godless fools. For these evil men dance to the tune of their demonic god Baal, quick to take by force of hand what is not theirs. They covet all, and take all with no remorse. They possess souls too small to understand the free bounty of God's graces and virtue. Fools they are, building impregnable castles of ignorance and hate upon the weak foundations of their souls. Forever defending themselves against heaven's graces.

Soon their temporal dark castles will fall under the return of heaven's light upon the earth. Only then will they see themselves as the devil's fools and slaves.

Demitasse

"Kama is the delight of body, mind and soul in exquisite sensation: awaken eyes, nose, tongue, ears, skin, and between sense and sensed, the essence of Kama will flower."
- Mallanaga Vatsyayana

My memory of her is without a doubt, and as I reminisce about her I can still feel her with all my senses. This was the moment of my fall, as she descended the loft stairway. She was dressed in chic hippy redux. She was wearing tight faded and frayed jeans that traced her perfectly shaped body, her shoulder-length hair caressed her cold shoulder H-line Boho spaghetti top, aflame in tie dye that trumped autumn's rainbow bloom. She was as subdued as wild and as sexy as innocent. Her well-formed body and chiseled Nordic face were flawless, she was the perfect divine proportion, living proof of the Fibonacci series I studied in architecture school.

As she walked off the stairway, she stopped for a moment and asked, "Do you like my outfit? I went shopping today, to pick out something I thought would take you back to your radical hippy days."

"Candy, your natural beauty exceeds the finest of exotic fabrics that flower the Earth."

"Roland, I want this to be a very special evening for both of us, one that we will remember with glee to the end of our days."

She took my hand, as I picked up my encased Stratocaster from the floor.

"Roland, this is our night ... a special night. We have both labored to overcome life's adversities. Tonight we will liberate ourselves together from the dark ... Right, Mr. Magnus?

"We will resurrect ourselves together, like the phoenix rising out of the ashes of defeat."

Her smile was as proportioned as the rest of her body. It was wide, spanning from ear to ear, like a pedestal that carried her facial aura now so clear and visible. In her aura I saw her past innocence and true heart, and the woman she had matured to now. It was an expanding radius of sexuality before me. I complimented her graciously, never compromising her femininity. I thought to myself, what a difference a day makes ... what an abyss twenty years-plus digs within my soul.

The moment was so Zen. As I gazed into her ocean blue eyes that reflected into my soul, that awakened my memory of my first rite of passage into my sexuality, as an early teen in the Sixties. She called me like those seductive and melodic voices of the sirens that inspired me to seduce my virginity. My memories were now draping one another – competing for dominance – as I felt her chakra's energy within me that uncoiled like an awakening serpent running throughout my soul ready to strike me with the venom of sexuality. Within a mere few seconds, which felt like an eternity, I drifted back on that moonless summer night, as I made love to Denise at her home by the pool. The memory of that evening, along with my now-awakened sexual energy, still run rampant within my carnal desires today. This new rite of passage, initiated my sexuality within my shadows of pleasure that consumed me like a purging fire, turning the dross of my virginity into sexual gold. For passion is such a great teacher, it's an inbred intellect and animalism that requires no mentor, requiring only one's hidden desires to be manifested in the flesh with a willing partner.

Every intimate detail of the surrendering of my virginity I recalled from the first kiss, foreplay and sexual alchemy. She was not inhibited, and very comfortable with her nakedness. Her long golden locks teased her naked shoulders, as the seductive playfulness of her large blue eyes invited me to her as no words can. I felt a sense of humble confidence, as I found pleasure in removing her bikini from her well-formed porcelain-skinned body, as we kissed and caressed and explored each other's now-exposed geography. I delighted in kissing her body from head to toes in a slow rhythmic motion as I turned her body. Her skin was soft, her body was scented with fluctuating goose bumps as I kissed her well-formed bosoms. My intellect consumed me as much as my flesh responded with rapture, while my hands freely explored her passions. The stillness of the night was only broken by her childlike giggles that reverberated our mutual orgasms. The beauty of youth is our naiveté that shields us from the reality of our sad mortality. As we played naked in her heated pool we completed our Varikrida.

The warm and clear October evening made al fresco dining possible in the rear courtyard of the restaurant. Candice reserved my favorite table in the corner affording us a clear and close view of the band. My good friend and guitarist extraordinaire Frank Martel's blues band, the Blue Haze, had the floor that night, having just returned from their East Coast tour. We started with a few drinks before dinner; Candy was sipping her red wine, while I succored my Absinthe – my drink of choice when I play out. Candy, and I engaged in inquisitive conversations ranging from theology, philosophy, psychology, and western esoteric Gnosticism. By 10 p.m. Demitasse was packed, as well as jumping with a full dance floor, with many of my fellow artists and intellectuals in attendance. Frank's band was now rockin' the house with a nonstop playlist of the best rockin' blues songs ever written, by the likes of B.B. King, Muddy Waters, Howlin Wolf, Willie Dixon, and John Lee Hooker, to name a few. By now Candy and I were gazing into each other's eyes, and taking our conversation into uncharted waters. Next I heard Frank make an announcement from the stage.

"We have a special guest with us this evening, my good friend and master of the Stratocaster ... blues man extraordinaire Roland Berengiere! So let's give him a strong round of applause as we welcome Roland on stage to join us, and to keep Demitasse rockin' til dawn."

I finished up my Absinthe, pulled my vintage Stratocaster from its case, and looked at Candy.

"See, I do keep my promises. Do you have a request?"

She got up from the table, and walked over to me to whisper her request in my ear ... and more. I jumped on stage, strapped on my guitar, and plugged in. I thanked the audience, and made my dedication.

"My first song is dedicated to a very special lady, and dear friend Candy."

I then jumped into my rendition of John Lee Hooker's Boom, Boom, Boom, adding a few original ripping guitar licks, then jumped into the lyrics with my gravelly blues voice, thanks to the Absinthe and Candy's sensual motivation. Her request was a self-fulfilling prophecy!

I was on a high roll, playing for about a good half-hour before turning the guitar work back to Frank, ending with another blues favorite of mine, *Caldonia*. By now everyone was on the dance floor. Candy grabbed me to join the dance melee, and we danced til midnight, holding each other tight and kissing oblivious to all in attendance. Candy then took my arm and whispered in my ear, saying she would like to head back to the loft while she was still on her energy high.

When we arrived at my loft, she was already feeling quite amorous. She lit some candles and incense, as she turned off the lights. Then asked me to play her favorite Donovan CD, starting with the song, *Hurdy Gurdy Man*. As I walked back to the open loft area, she looked at me most seductively, then in a very soft seductive voice she whispered into my ear ... She started singing along with the song.

As she was singing her song most seductively, Candy began to strip for me in the most erotic seduction I had ever experienced in my life. She slowly untied the spaghetti strings of her halter top, exposing the black lace bra she was wearing. Next she kicked off her moccasins, then slowly started to unzip and unbutton her jeans letting them fall to the floor as she danced in slow motion exposing her black lace thong, and beautiful well-formed legs, then turning around as she gyrated sharing the vision of her well-formed and tight butt. Next she pulled her bandana from her head and started to swing it around her in a slow surreal motion. She then wrapped it about her hips, covering her thong, then letting her thong drop to the floor, then took off her bra, revealing her upright and perfect bosoms. Next she dropped her bandana from her curved hips, exposing her shaved yoni. She took her bandana and wrapped it around her wrists as she approached me, to undress me. I pulled the flower from hair. She slowly undressed me, as my senses came alive to the delight of my body, mind and soul. My eyes, nose, tongue, ears, skin united as I felt her soft skin, touched her fragranced hair, as our probing hands shared no boundaries, as our mouths united in bliss, we were now two with interchangeable roles of the hunter and its prey.

In maturity we learn to cherish and embrace the rapture of prolonged lovemaking that affords us a mutual orgasm of the flesh and soul, unlike in our youth when lovemaking was reduced to a short-lived physical thrill. She was a fast learner of the sexual arts and sexual alchemy. We learned to respect and nourish our serpent energy, known as the Kundalini by the ancient Hindus, an energy that runs through the chakras of our flesh and spirit and stretches our desires to couple our naked bodies as one. An energy that heals with each thrust of passion, as it unwinds itself in foreplay to expose our vulnerabilities to our passionate lover, seeking the strength of our weaknesses to strike back with the power of submissiveness.

She laid on my bed naked on her stomach calling me silently and without movement. Her skin was flawless, without blemish, tight and soft. She whispered, professor teach me the *Kama Sutra*, I am a simple country girl seeking to find her sexuality without having to be labeled a whore.

To be a practitioner of the *Kama Sutra*, Candy, one must first think like a writer, thinking first about their psalms of seduction before they can share their story with their partner. We must first purge ourselves of our latent sexisms if we truly want to surrender to the higher power of love that makes us rise above our constructed egos that breed our insecurities, which suppress our higher senses."

I then started to softly touch her body, first her inner thighs, then explored her body with my tongue and mouth, kissing her neck ... then working my way down her back, to the fold of her butt, to her now-spread legs. I then turned her over, as I would a page of the *Kama Sutra*, in anticipation of delight that each new page would bring. I could feel her passions in her sweet breath with each kiss and caress. Our passions were aroused spreading from chakra to chakra. Starting at the base of the spine the Kundalini spiraled through us now coiled and ready to strike. The Adepts know that controlling their unleashed Kundalini will lead them to salvation – achieving Moksha – the release from the cycle of life and death.

I then directed my carnal journey down the path of her body, one I would often repeat, softly kissing her bosoms, stomach, naval as my hand stimulated her yoni, bringing her to her first orgasm. Her delight was found in the truth of her silent face that was bathed in her aura; for words need not to confirm what the soul already knows. She placed her hand on my lingam as she released her feminine joy. Then began an act of nominal congress.

True practitioners of the *Kama Sutra* consider sex as a natural necessity, almost to the point of sacramental. The *Kama Sutra* is not a sex manual, nor pornographic, it is something much deeper. It is a work of art, requiring the practitioners to approach their lovers on multiple levels of satisfaction from the physical, philosophical, metaphysical, to the spiritual. We were like Shiva, and his wife goddess Pravati, locked away in our palace on Mount Kailash. In our lovemaking we annihilated time, we were living in a fine moment of eternity. Our lovemaking flowed like a song with each kiss and caress adding new notes for a new crescendo to reach.

With affection we washed each other under the streams of pulsating water, tantalizingly teasing each other, building our appetite for more intense pleasures to come. We then engaged in our Varikrida – the water game, embraced in our lovemaking in the shower. We washed and explored each other's intimate flesh, to purge and purify our skin and souls, and to release the dark memories of our past lovers. Then gently we toweled ourselves off to prepare for our mutual surrenders. I laid her down on her stomach on the bed. I gently messaged her back, buttocks, and the backs of her legs with jasmine and bergamot oils. We then engaged in the myriad of lovemaking positions, as we regulated the rhythm of our breathing with slow deep breaths that prolonged our lovemaking till the first light of dawn. We then caressed as we drifted into our mutual sleep.

THE TAKE-OFF

I helped her with her packing, and loaded the suitcases into my SUV, as she was getting dressed. When she emerged from my loft, she was talking on her cell, looking a little confused.

"Sorry, Roland, that was my attorney I was speaking with. I hate to impose again, can we stop by his office on the way to the airport?"

"Sure, we have time, is there a problem?"

"Ummh not really, you know how these divorces go, there is always some small detail overlooked until the last moment. All will be fine."

On our way to the Westchester County Airport, I drove to her lawyer's office in White Plains. She was in good hands, having retained a rather prestigious law firm, run by one of the most aggressive divorce attorneys in the area – Arnold Cribari. When she emerged from his office, she looked as if she had left her glowing aura at the door.

"Everything alright Candy?"

"For sure, Roland, just a bit of a delay in the final settlement."

"Fret not, Candy, you retained the best attorney money can buy."

"Roland, looks like we are good on time, do you mind driving me to the Westchester Mall, I want to pick up a few gifts for my parents. I will be quick; to save time would you be able to pick up coffee at the food court? I will meet you there. She returned about a half hour later with a few shopping bags in hand. "OK, Roland, I am ready, we still have some time before my flight leaves, and we should make it in time, without rushing."

"What are your plans for the future, Candy?"

"Well, I will have to take care of my parents for a while until my brother arrives after the first of the year. My parents are not aging well; my mother has dementia, and my father is recovering from a triple bypass surgery. As part of the divorce agreement, we have to sell our house in East Fishkill. When it is sold I will be returning to Dutchess to settle my affairs. I plan to complete my MBA in Westchester County or back in Idaho, depending on what happens over the next few months. Roland, isn't it just fascinating how our lives crossed paths? You really have me thinking about mysticism and the occult. Did I tell you how I took your class more by accident? I was scheduled to take a course in sociology, but it was cancelled due to lack of enrollment. So my guidance counselor informed me your class was still open, and there were no overrides pending, so I enrolled. Don't let it go to your head; a lot of students spoke rather highly of you. Just think, we may have never met and experienced our unplanned week of romance."

"I agree, we lived our fantasies by failing to daydream of the mundane. You held the autumn of my life in abeyance, affording me the time to take a few last breaths of my youth."

"Roland, do you love me?"

"My soul loves you, as my heart will miss you, far more than my flesh can deliver, and my poems express."

"Roland, I will be back as soon as the house is sold. I will stay with you, and share in your new artist and bohemian lifestyle. Well, we are almost at the gate. Here, Roland, this is a little gift for all you have done for me. Please do not open it until you arrive home, it pales compared to the joys you shared with me, and all you taught me about life. Also, Roland, please promise me this, do not forsake my request. I want you to know and remember me for my character, for I do not lay with any man, or would do so just to satisfy my desire of the flesh. Roland, I will never lie to you knowingly, nor compromise your virtue. Please?"

"Candy, what are you trying to tell me?"

"Roland, I love you more, and have never loved another man as much as I have loved you. Please understand the emotions of my beating, loving heart; and my earnest love I have for you has outpaced the slow injustice of an adulterer. Roland, time will heal and correct all of the wrongs of our past. Got to run, we are at the gate. Just one more sweet kiss before we leave each other. Not sure when I will be back. Will call to let you know I arrived safe!"

I waited in the parking lot, watching and waiting until her plane taxied and took off. It was an unseasonably cold October day, the sky was grey, and the once forest of rainbow trees were now bare, exposing their contorted limbs. A low-flying raven crossed my windshield as I entered Route 84 from King Street. A sense of melancholy overcame me, like never before. I turned on my radio to an oldies station – my only route to the foreign land of the past – trying to find a groove to make me feel right. As my mind returned from the land of the will-o-wisps, I became conscious of the song playing. It was in the groove, very Zen, it was synchronicity at work; I sang along to the Lovin Spoonful's, *Younger Girl*. In my new-found happiness, a sense of melancholy breached my soul for the first time in my life. It was not a depressed feeling … rather a fear of the unknown. I began to accept my future had arrived ahead of time. It was a chilling call from the wilderness of my soul.

Upon arriving home, I received the call I was expecting from the Roseland Medical Center."

Speaking. Yes I am free to talk. Huummmh, well it is no surprise, we were expecting this for some time. I understand. I will schedule my follow-up appointment with you ASAP to discuss the next steps. Thank you, Dr. Kraft."

As I was going through my mail, I opened a letter from my attorney, believing it was just another overinflated bill. It was a letter informing me one of my biggest clients had filed for bankruptcy, and listed me as the sixth lien holder, advising me they can only offer twenty cents on the dollar and no compensation for legal costs. The next letter I opened contained my attorney's bill. To be paid in full for services rendered.

I received a text from Candy later in the day, informing me she arrived safely, and was looking for a reunion in the near future. I went upstairs to reclaim my bedroom loft, finding Candy's hippy wardrobe neatly pressed and folded on the bed, next to her sexy lingerie, with a small handwritten note.

Dear Roland,
I thought it best to leave these here for when I return for another week of romance, dinners and dancing at Demitasse.
Love,
Candy

After returning home from dinner with a few of my friends, I unwrapped Candy's gift, which included a number of blues CDs, a book on the blues, and a *Kama Sutra* she signed, along with a folded note inside. After reading it I just crumpled it up, and threw it across the floor. The past is a foreign land one can never return to, though we will be judged by our sins of yesterday by an unforgiving present that will transcend us by projecting our sins to a future without us.

YOUR WIFE, MY FRIEND, OUR PROBLEM

My daydream of Candy was broken by a cell phone call.

"Hey, Roland, it's Rebecca. What are you up to? Have not heard from you in a while."

"Hi Rebecca, I'm at Karen's Kitchen in Cold Spring. Sipping coffee, watching life go by, with pen and paper in hand."

"What time you planning to be home, Roland?"

"Say around 5-ish, have to run a few errands, then have to meet up with my good architect friend, Michael, to discuss a new project, why?"

"Well, do you have any plans for dinner?"

"Well, aside from eating – none."

"Well, I'm hoping to stop by your place, then I thought we can go to that new Thai restaurant down the street from your loft. Just to talk, and catch up on life. O, by the way, do you have a houseguest? Would hate to piss off your girlfriend – Nancy. Hey, Roland, how about if I come over dressed really hot and sexy, just to make her jealous – you can do better than Nancy. I am telling you Roland, as a woman, you are right, there is something Nancy is hiding from you. And, I can help you get rid of her ... will be easy work ... I do have an excellent reputation, and track record for poaching. It's an easy way to rid yourself of her."

"You don't have to worry about that, Rebecca – I just broke up with her over the past weekend."

"Huumhhhh, really! Well this is no surprise, you told me you had an uneasy feeling about her since you met her. Well, Roland, one woman's loss is another woman's gain. Well, I guess I can come dressed for the occasion. I'll stop by around 5-ish to share some Absinthe together."

"Sure, Rebecca; before I forget, how is your husband, Tim, doing?"

"O, he is doing fine, he is working late tonight on some project. So he suggested I call you, and make plans to take you out for dinner. It's his chaperone money. He knows you're a solid guy, and a great friend, and helped us through some tough emotional times, and besides he trusts you, being old enough to be my dad ... ha-ha. And, you will keep me away from my demons."

"Ha-ha, this is no easy task, Rebecca."

As expected, Rebecca dropped in on time, dressed as planned in a tight-fitting black dress with a liberal hemline and a neckline to match, nylon stockings to cover her long legs, carried by her stilettos. Her light brown hair was a bit wild, resting on her shoulders, and her face angelic to cover her devilish intentions.

"So, Roland, a toast to your new-found freedom, for ridding yourself of that Nancy bitch. Welcome back to bachelorhood. Pass that Absinthe. And, excuse me Roland, I will need to shower and wash my hair. I love this open plan living."

"Do you think Tim will have an issue with this?"

"O, Roland, come on now, he knows you are an artist, and not the inhibited type."

She undressed then jumped into the shower, lathered up and washed her hair, as she continued on with her conversation.

"Roland, where the hell is that Absinthe, and please get me a towel."

She took the towel wrapped it around her head, while

ascending the steps to my loft, what a sight! – My senses were on overload.

"Hey, Roland," she shouted from the loft. "Hot lingerie, a parting gift and memento from Nancy, hell she does have good taste. You must share this story with me over dinner. Hell, if they're not Nancy's, who the hell's are they … hell! – You work fast, Roland. I wish Tim had your energy and stamina, and he is five years my junior. See what happens when you get married, your sex life melts away like snow in July. Hey, Roland, mind if I try it on, maybe I should take it home and put it on for Tim, and see how he responds."

"I would, not recommend that."

"Why Roland, he trusts you."

"He won't after you tell him it was from me, and I thought you looked quite sexy in it. Besides, he owns a few guns."

"O, Roland, chill out."

She then came downstairs. As I was going through my mail, I looked out my window.

"Hey, Roland! Surprise … don't I look hot, desirable and fuckable … hey Roland? You ever fuck anyone's wife? You know have a Cinq à Sept?"

My expression turned cold … .I was unable to talk for a moment …

"Roland … what's the matter, Mr. Moralist, can't admit you could have a nice tumble with someone's wife, just for the adventure?"

"Rebecca, come now, we are friends. Let's not ruin the evening, you know my position on this."

"Hey Roland, chill out, just having a little fun with you. Hey, did you ever do your ex, just for the fun of it?"

"Hell, Rebecca, I never had sex with my wife for the fun of it when I was married to her! A man never goes back to sip vinegar once he has tasted honey."

"O, Roland, have you no taste for my honey?"

"Hey, Rebecca, you're going to have to shake your ass, we are going to be late for dinner; I have reservations for 6:30."

"Roland, do I have a better ass than Nancy?"

"No contest."

"Well, how does it compare to your new paramour's ass?"

"It's a draw."

"Well, fuck you, Roland."

"Hey, Rebecca, I should not be looking at your ass in the raw, or commenting on the ass of a married woman."

"O, Roland, don't play that Puritan game with me. Are you telling me women can't have a nice ass after they are married? Huuhh Roland?"

"Rebecca, sure they can, how else are they to keep their husbands from straying? But it is their husbands who should be giving the compliment, not a friend of their husband."

"O, Roland, looks like you had a lot of fun this weekend. I am sure you did not just hold hands. Tell me more."

"Rebecca, over dinner."

"I want to hear it, not from a secondary source."

I reserved my favorite table with the window view of the Hudson. "Roland, do they serve Absinthe here?"

"No Rebecca, you are going to have to do with the house stock."

"Waiter, please bring the table a bottle of your best 1998 vintage Malbec from the Highland's winery."

"A good choice, you know how to choose your wines, madam."

"And, my men, too."

"Yes, I see you have a preference for the aged and vintage."

"Roland, you know I really enjoy your company. You are

quite interesting, very knowledgeable, and you are such a mystery, and contradiction. You know, I really love Tim, though you will not believe this having known me over the past years, especially with all my baggage. But he is not very enlightened, not an ounce of artist's blood in him. If it were not for you taking me to the jazz concerts, classical performances at the Bardavon – remember the Yo Yo Ma concert, and dinner at the CIA, and those blues shows at Demitasse, I would have no real social life. Sometimes I believe he is becoming bored with me."

"Rebecca, I do not believe you could bore any man."

"Roland, you know well and understand the demons I have been fighting all my life. You also know I got my life together after talking to you, taking your advice. I went back to college, received my nursing degree, have been on the wagon since I met you, I have even been faithful to Tim."

"So, Rebecca, I see you are drinking again, what triggered this?"

"Roland, you know I tell you everything, and hide no secrets. But I am starting to feel lonely again, I have a fear of aging. I am thirty-five years old, and feeling lost in my marriage to Tim. He has no zest for life, like you, Roland."

"O, sorry for the pity party, I wanted to catch up with you to see how things were going with Nancy. I know you never had a good feeling for her. So what's the story?"

"The short of it all is that she has a drinking, gambling addiction, and I caught her having sex with her ex-husband for money to pay off her debts."

"Well, hell, Roland, at least give her credit for being entrepreneurial. See, Roland, you don't get it, the Cinq à Sept thing, it is so common and fashionable. I don't understand how an intellectual guy with so much worldly experience believes in fidelity – especially in these times. What gives, Roland? Your loft is always decorated with women's sexy lingerie? Does a fucking piece of paper make women less desirable to you?"

"No, Rebecca, my respect for fidelity does not blind me to a woman's beauty and charm. It only affords me to know and feel the cost of infidelity. One should never dream and chase a fantasy they do not belong in. How would you feel if Tim was having a Cinq à Sept?"

"O, Roland, I hate when you pull this golden rule shit on me, with all your balanced moral logic. Hell, Roland, if I caught Tim in an affair, and he offered me the option of saving our marriage, allowing me the right to have an affair with a man of my choice – hell yeah – the golden rule ... right Roland? And, I chose you, would you have an affair with me then!"

"No, Rebecca, you would still be married, and living in a world of reprisals for a perceived justice."

"Roland, you must have brass balls, the restraint of a saint, or be the biggest fucking fool I ever met!"

"Rebecca, guilty as charged, what is my sentence?"

"O, Roland, not getting into my fucking pussy!"

"I would not want to lose our friendship over a piece of ass. Does not your heart love a true friend more?"

"O, Roland, now you are fucking with my head!"

"Check mate – Rebecca."

"O, Roland, I know, you're right. Well does a blow ... "

"Rebecca, please."

"Fuck you, brass balls, where do you go to get them polished?" She broke the tension, and conversation.

"So back to Nancy, was she good in bed? She was hot looking for a forty-five year old. I only met her once, at one of your gallery exhibits – she looked fucking bored, or too stupid to understand and appreciate your work. Hey, was she good in bed, and into that Kama stuff you talk about?"

"Well, good in bed? An "A" for trying, but not very satisfying. She was oblivious to the *Kama Sutra*, and Tantric lovemaking. After the break up, I was informed she is also a sex addict, she just wanted it quick and fast … to satisfy the high of her bipolar condition. We had nothing in common to talk about, so her sexuality was as short as her conversations. What is there left to do with each other for a weekend in the mountains? I found out she only earned a GED, while in rehab, she also had a few DWIs she never told me about, and two ex-husbands!"

"So how did it end – Roland, would love to hear how you extracted yourself out of this one without the drama."

"To get to the short of it, she fell off the wagon over the past week, unbeknownst to me. So as we planned our two-month anniversary … "

"O, Roland, I must interject here to kick you in your fucking brass intellectual balls. Two fucking months! Well this is a record for you."

"Well, I found her drunk, naked, sleeping and snoring in bed, when I returned from getting our luggage. I then fetched her ex-husband, drunk and semi-conscience, from the bar. I walked him to the room and sat him down on the bed, closed the door, and left them there. I went to check out and pay my tab, only to find they charged the entire bar tab to my account."

"Hey, fuck, man, how much did this set you back? I mean, just a night at the Rhinebeck Hotel is big bucks."

"For sure, over a thousand dollars, though in hindsight I got away cheap and without the drama."

"Well, did you at least get laid?"

"No."

"Roland, why, she was drunk – you could have had one last parting shot."

"What pleasure is there in having sex with an unconscious

woman? It would be like fucking the dead. And, besides, if I dropped my brass balls into her polluted well, I would be having them rust-coated today."

We both laughed, then Tim called to see how she was doing.

"Hey, Tim, all is well. I am here with Roland. We are going to some Thai restaurant in Beacon, talking about how his dating scene is going. Hey, Roland, Tim sends his best. He wants us to get together for dinner with your lady friend."

"Pass on my best to Tim. Tell him when life settles down for me we will all get together."

"OK, Tim, well, things never seem to slow down for Roland. We will work something out, will talk later, what time you planning to be home? Love ya."

"Are you going to share with me who this new mystery woman is? She has a refined taste for lingerie."

"And men, too."

"O, for sure, Roland. Do you have a picture of her?"

"Sure, I have a few on my cell, what do you think?"

"Hey, Roland, she looks rather young, and quite attractive. How old is she, robbing the cradle, old man?"

"She is a former student of mine. She flew into town from Idaho to take care of some legal matters."

"How long did she stay at your place?"

"About a week or so."

"Looks like you two had quite a romantic roundelay. Was it planned?"

"Not really, just synchronicity at work."

"Why, Roland, she is so young and beautiful; this is so unlike you, especially getting involved with your students, and a younger woman."

"Well, a former student."

"O, Roland, does this allow you to change your steadfast

rules? Roland, tell me if you were in bed with her, and she whispered in your ear she was married, would you throw her out of bed in the heat of your passions?"

"O, Rebecca, this is such an unfair question."

"Well, Roland, you look a little disturbed?"

"No, Rebecca, just a little tired. Time to head back."

"Hey, Roland, you look down. How about going back to your place for one last Absinthe?"

Back at the loft Rebecca was enjoying the Absinthe, as she cozied herself on my expansive couch.

"Hey, Roland, I still can't figure you out, your existential/ Gnostic ennui confuses me. Your disciplined morality seems like a contraction to me – On one hand you say you don't get involved with married women – or even women involved in relationships. You hold fast that you do not get between lovers, nor step on another man's turf. On the grounds that you do not play with someone's emotions for personal gain? Right, Roland?"

"This is correct, Rebecca?"

"So what is the bigger sin, Roland? Not to get involved with a married woman – even in a poor marriage – for the sake of fidelity? Or denying a married woman who needs your love – leaving her in a time of her emotional need? Is not the latter, not only playing with her emotions – or just outright killing them? Does this not unsettle your self-righteous soul?"

"Yes, Rebecca, you are right. But will I leave her in an improved emotional state if I have sex with her for a quick fix, only then to have her face the emotional crisis of committing adultery, leaving her in conflict to choose between me – who has no plans for a long-term relationship – and her husband, and have her lie straight-faced in her husband's eyes about her fidelity? In each case, our emotions are compromised, though by inserting a third party, I will only expand the radius of the lying. With now three damaged emotions."

She then walked over to the table and prepared another Absinthe. As she did this, she slipped out of her sexy black dress, now only wearing her lace panty and bra, complete with her stiletto shoes. She retook her position on the couch, crossing her long beautiful legs.

"Roland, I still don't accept it, you make sex out to be larger than it really is. For example, if I just undressed in front of you for the sake of having sex, and you penetrate me for some quick fun, what is the big deal? I get dressed and go home, like nothing has happened. Nobody knows, and we both go on with our lives, knowing we had great sex together. I will still be married to Tim, less miserable and satisfied, and you can go on fucking your student paramour. Nothing has changed, Roland, except raising the bar of our happiness."

"She stood up and removed her bra and panty, and walked over to me. She was of tall German stock, and the stilettos added to her 5-foot 8-inch frame, though by now staggering from all the Absinthe and wine. She planted herself next to me sitting on the floor.

"So what is it, am I right or not?"

"Rebecca, you are a radical atheist, adverse to the notion of mortals having an eternal soul. For you, no sin or guilt exists if you are not found out. Your "god" is merely a shallow epicurean series of non-ending pleasures, limited only to the worthiness of your lies and manipulations."

"Roland, I just can't fathom how a brilliant existentialist and philosopher like you can think in such parochial ways. Hey, Mr. Christian, wasn't it Jesus who saved the prostitute from being stoned to death for adultery? Isn't your God an all-merciful God? Did your Messiah err? What about all the stories in your Holy

Books about forgiveness and love? Tell me honestly, Roland, do you fear God? Or is your ego so fucking big, you really believe you can compete with God?" And, besides, you are no fucking celibate, how many women house guests do you share your bed with? The lacy lingerie did not fall to your bed from heaven!"

She then nuzzled up to me placed one arm around me, drawing me closer to her lips, then took my hand and placed it between her legs, gave me a French kiss, then whispered into my ear, "See Roland, you are truly a saint, you now have your hand planted in heaven; now don't make a martyr out of yourself, just fuck me now!"

"Rebecca, now stop it, get hold of yourself, we have to get you back on the wagon."

"So, you won't fuck me, Roland. Hell, you fucking hypocrite, you have had a number of frequent and rather nice sexual liaisons with my older sister for the past few years! You fuck her but not me … is this another of your fucking moral conundrums? You do like playing with women's emotions, don't you? And, what do you do with my sister that you can't tell me, and do with me?"

"Rebecca, please, a gentleman does not kiss and tell."

"Well, don't tell me then, I will ask my sister myself. Besides, I like her versions better, she never edits … and, besides, she also told me about the ménage á trois with her and her friend. Roland, do you think Jesus would intercede for you being stoned for the fucking whore you really are?"

"Rebecca, please listen. You are off the wagon and your meds. You know where you wound up the last time you went in this direction. You have a great job, a future, and a great husband – why forsake it, Rebecca, for me?"

"Roland, why can't we just sleep together tonight, what is the real harm? Roland, who will get hurt, I am the victim?"

"Yes, Rebecca, at this moment you are the victim of an insidious disorder. But we both know if we entertain this, we will both be cheating on your husband and sister. You are wise enough to know this. We will find bliss as lovers for a mere evening, only to forsake our friendship, and hate each other for the rest of our lives."

She stood herself up and while walking to the bathroom she threw up all over herself, and my new furniture. I took her arm and walked her to the lower-floor bathroom, to purge her stomach of all the Absinthe. When she exited she gave me a big hug, and said, "Thank you Roland, I am sorry for all the things I said to you."

"What are friends for, Rebecca? I prepared a shower for you, and I will steady you so you don't fall. She lathered herself up, and washed her hair. When she was finished, I gave her one of my robes, and walked her upstairs to the loft bedroom. I unmade the bed, dropped her in bed, pulled the covers over her, and said, "Goodnight Rebecca, you will be OK. If you need me, I will be downstairs on the couch sleeping. Now get some rest."

It was around 1 a.m. in the morning when Tim called.

"Hi, Roland, is Rebecca still at your place? I am still at work, I am up for a promotion, and a possible new assignment on the West Coast that will require relocating."

"I am glad to hear this, the move would be great for your career, and for you and Rebecca. She had a tough evening, Tim, you know she fell off the wagon?"

"Yes I know, she was doing so good. She started drinking again a few days ago, so I thought I would have her come and talk to you over dinner. You seem to know how to handle her."

"Well, thanks, Tim. She had a bit too much to drink, then started to get sick; it is best to keep her off the road. I put her to bed up in the loft, and she is in a deep sleep. Do you want to come over after work, and crash here for the night?"

"No need to, she is in good hands, just send her home when it is safe for her to drive."

"Better yet, alcohol stays in the bloodstream for quite a while. When she wakes up, I will just drive her home, and you guys can come by later to pick up her car. It's in my guest parking slip, so the car won't get towed."

"Sorry for all the headaches, Roland.

"No problem, now go make some money for that down payment on your house on the West Coast."

In the morning I took Rebecca to a local café for espresso – she was still rather shit-faced – before I drove her home. She was not in a talkative mood.

"Roland, how did Tim take it, is he mad at me, do you think I am going to lose him?"

"No Rebecca he took it in good order."

"You did not tell him of my exhibition and behavior – did you?"

"No, Rebecca, we are both very concerned about you. You will need to get yourself back in therapy, and start taking your meds again. I think the West Coast will be good for you guys. I will drop you off at your place, and you and Tim can drive down later in the day to pick up your car."

"What are your plans for the near future, Roland, will I see you over the holidays?"

"Well, my art exhibition opens December 1st at the Foundry Art Gallery in Beacon; the opening is a black-tie affair. I have two complimentary tickets for you and Tim as my guests. It will be an exciting evening for us. The proceeds from the art auction will be donated to the Alexandria Foundation in Quakertown, PA, for the construction of a new private school for preparing students for the Great Work to assist our humanity in distress. Than after the holidays I will be heading out to PA for a spiritual retreat of sorts, and my follow-up visit to the Roseland Healing Center."

"What's going on Roland, is everything all right?"

"Things could not be better, Rebecca, I am just reengineering myself to transition into my next career."

"O, Roland, you always talk in riddles. You love mystery and to keep people in suspense. Well, we look forward to seeing you at your opening, and, hey, please call us to keep us informed of what is going on in your life."

"Well here we are, get a little rest, will talk soon."

"Roland, you never told me, are you planning on seeing that cute student of yours? I would love to meet her."

Later in the day I received a call from Roseland Medical confirming the dates for my next round of blood work, MRIs and consultation with the surgical team. I did not return Candy's text.

What Are Friends For?

I was looking forward to spending time again with Candy; it had been a year since I dropped her off at the airport. Though her note caused me quite some consternation, and a feeling of betrayal. I would be in denial not to admit I missed her company dearly over the past year. She was the last true summer breeze that rustled the few remaining golden leaves of my soul in the autumn of my life. I wondered how many more winters lay ahead of me.

I looked back to my past life with indifference, for it is a foreign land, one to which I could never return. For what I am today is merely an anthology of my past decisions, and the consequences it has rendered me. In retrospect, I have not found favor with all of my worldly accomplishments, rather dissatisfaction for what I have failed to achieve. I have been wise in my ways – to a respectable degree – to avoid sins of commission, though equally ignorant in understanding my sins of omission. I have little tolerance for ignorance, and less for self-pity. I have turned my back with indignation against modern society's contorted yardstick for measuring one's success. Being wise enough to see through the illusions that one's character, talents, and intelligence are not determined by one's zip code. I have valued the beauty of natural and manmade aesthetics, over the ugliness and vanity of pop culture.

My self-psychoanalysis was broken by the sound of the cleaning lady I had retained to keep my loft intact, and to ready it for the number of guests who were scheduled to visit over the coming few weeks. I had been busy over the last year with teaching, consulting, my artwork and music. Not to mention lawyers, accountants, Roseland Medical Center and serving on the board of directors at the Alexandria Foundation.

After the cleaning lady left, Beth emerged from the loft, still half asleep, and jumped into the shower.

"Hey, Roland! Pass me the shampoo, the body soap and a towel. I overslept again. You were supposed to wake me up! We have a long and busy day ahead."

She dressed, and was preparing to take care of the day's errands.

"So, Roland, what's the plan, we have a tight schedule."

"Take my credit card, and pick out a classy evening dress for your sister. You know Rebecca's taste in clothing. I want you to surprise her with it. And also get her shoes and accessories. This is a special black-tie event, held at the La Chanson Art Gallery, after the auction."

"Roland, I promise I will pick out the most seductive outfit I find."

"Beth, don't make it too sexy, Rebecca is coming as my guest."

"Hey, Roland, I can handle the competition, even if it's my younger sister. And, besides, I am staying at your place tonight, and you are dropping her off at the house."

"Hey, Beth, you OK with this?"

"Roland, we are sisters, we talk a lot, and she shared the story about the exhibition she presented you with, and how you deflected it."

"How much do you share with her about us?"

"Just about everything, Roland! Sibling rivalry at its best."

"After you take care of that, go see the caterer to make the final menu selection for Tim and Rebecca's farewell party, as well."

"Hey, Roland, you forgetting something'?

"Most Likely – What?"

"Well, how about a nice outfit for me?"

"Sure – no limits on sexy on this one."

"Hey Beth, can you man my business phone as I shower? I am expecting a few important calls that need attention."

"Sure, Roland! Should I take a message, or are you are taking your calls?"

"Please just take the message; you can tell by the tone of their voice if it is important, hostile or friendly."

As Roland dressed, Beth was busy taking calls.

"Are you ready, Beth? Any calls?"

"A few, one from Dr. Kraft from Roseland Medical, The Alexandria Foundation, Bob Kelly your banker, and some real nasty guy, Mr. Ganelon. Why is the Roseland Medical Center calling you, Roland?"

"What do you think? – looking for donors."

Beth headed out to do her shopping, as I used the day to catch up on paperwork and call on a few clients, though I fell short on both tasks. My mind just drifted back to fond memories with Candy. I was projecting in my head how this reunion would go. I was trying to rationalize her intent, and actions. Was she sincere, also a victim, or looking for emotional payback? Candy's departing note had shaken the foundation of my morality. Time will heal all wounds, after all life is merely a diversion from death.

Rebecca looked stunning as she entered the gallery. Beth had done her homework well. By the time she caught up with me she already had a glass of champagne in her hand. This event was a bit out of her normal social circles. She was born and raised in a factory town, on the other side of the tracks, somewhere upstate.

She had a difficult life, one she had most earnestly shared with me most candidly, unscripted and unedited. She looked more mature than her thirty-five years, in her sophisticated attire. Over the past few years of our friendship she made it clear how important it was to her to actually attend such an event. Tonight I was honoring her wish, before she and Tim left for the West Coast. He finally squirreled away enough money to buy their dream house in Oregon.

"Hey, Roland, Thanks for the nice outfit, I was not expecting it, and I thought I would have to borrow something nice to attend such a formal art event. Roland, you really have me believing in this synchronicity stuff. After all, we met for the first time at the Rhinebeck Gallery, at the opening of your exhibit. Do you remember?"

"O, quite well, Rebecca."

"Looking back, it was quite an amusing encounter. It was the first time I attended such an event, I really felt out of place – very self-conscious of my background ... to the point of feeling inferior. You know, all those uppity artists and socialites all dressed up. Then, after you greeted the crowd, and talked about your minimalist and existential works, I just went up to you as you and asked if I could get you a drink, and inquired about your preference ... I was happily surprised to hear it was Absinthe – synchronicity ... right? Do you remember how we talked all evening, as they auctioned off your work? Then, heading out to Demitasse, to meet up with your artist friends. Then I remember you stopped talking abruptly, and injected the non sequitur – 'For heaven's sake, are you married, or involved in a relationship?' Remember, when I said I have been living with my boyfriend for three years, your response?"

"How can I forget, 'Does he approve of this?'"

"Now, how ironic is this, Roland? Here we are five years

later, and now married to Tim, and he asks you to take me to this event to live a life dream."

"Rebecca, you need to dream bigger dreams, and live your life bigger than your dreams."

"True, Roland, I never imagined myself ever owning a house in Oregon, to receive a B.S. in Nursing and pass my RN license."

"You have come a long way over the past few years; you should be proud of yourself, Rebecca."

"Hey, Roland, after the show, how about if we go to Demitasse for some Absinthe, one last time before I head to a new life on the West Coast."

"Drinks on me, Rebecca."

"Roland, remember all those great conversations we had here, religion, philosophy, and all our intimate conversations we shared till the wee hours of the morning? I love your poetry ... really turns me on. I have to thank you for being such a loyal and trusted friend, and all the support you gave me as I was trying to overcome my demons. Getting me to enroll in college, writing letters of recommendation, and, of course, those evenings when I came knocking at your door in the middle of the night, too shit-faced to drive home – looking to crash at your place – I know that pissed your girlfriends off."

"Well, for sure, Rebecca, what explanation can I possibly give my lady friend when you come over drunk, take your clothes off and jump in the shower right in front of us? Then turn around and tell her, 'Don't worry, it's OK, I do it all the time?'"

"Well, Roland, I was not lying, and you are the moralist who never lies. The problem is, Roland, they never believed the truth. Well, I am truly sorry, but look at the memories we created together – think of us as celibate lovers. I am sure your artist friends are all thinking we are at your loft making passionate love, and you are cheating on Beth ... wait till you tell them I'm her sister! Hell, Roland, either I am going to totally ruin your reputation before I head out, or make you some kind of hero"

"Well, Rebecca, this will most likely be the last time we speak in private. There will be little time at the farewell party I am throwing for you and Tim next week, so if you have anything to share with me, or have any questions, we should discuss them now. I know there are a few matters troubling you, Rebecca, and if you fail to address them you may lapse into a serious depression, and run to your demons to get you out, only to have them bury you."

"Roland, you have been my confidant for the past few years. I shared with you my story of coming to age prematurely. How my father physically abused me as a child, to the point where my mother and I had to get a restraining order to get him out of the house. He would come home drunk, and just start beating me for no reason. When he left my mother with little means of support, we lived in rent subsidized apartments. I was only fourteen years old, watching my mother struggle to support my two sisters and brother. To help relieve her burdens, I left home and got involved with an older guy who took me in. I was just looking for someone to love me, he was my father figure and lover. You know the story, he got me pregnant, and one day just left. I was forced to move back in with my mother.

"When my son was born, I was just fifteen, and I could not abandon the child as my father did to us. I was not in any condition to raise this child, so I let my mother raise him. Feeling guilty about adding more burden on my mother, I started to sell myself on the street, making good money, and able to help support the household, then becoming addicted to drugs and sex, not to mention my alcoholism. I eventually went to seek help, cleaned myself up, left my son with my mother to raise, and moved to Fishkill with some old friends to start a new life. I never shared this with Tim, and we are now married, moving up in the world. I can't afford to lose him. Now I am in conflict, hiding my past from him, along with my son. All of these years with Tim, he has never met him. I told Tim he is my younger brother. How should I handle this, Roland?"

"You have gotten yourself in a tough spot, Rebecca."

"Can you blame me? Here I was a total loser, former drug addict, sex addict and alcoholic, who finally comes across Mr. Right. He is handsome, five years my junior, a good job, with a great future. If I told him the truth, he never would have taken me seriously. I could not afford to lose him – I truly love him. How long can I keep this from him – especially my son? When my son visits us, how can I deny my own son?"

"See, Rebecca, see – you do have a conscience that wants to do right – you are maturing now, you will need to take ownership of this."

"How, Roland, and when?"

"Has Tim ever shared his past experiences with you?"

"He has, though to be honest, they were rather innocent."

"Your story is quite moving, and your actions were based out of circumstance, and the need to survive. Your father beat you as a child, you were held hostage, you had no one to help and love you. So you found an older man, to be your surrogate father, and to give you the love and affection never rendered by your father. Then had a child with him; you elected to bring the child into the world, and not abort him. And now you have a beautiful son to love, as he loves you. Tim will understand this. He has always been supportive of you – all the time, to a fault. He knows of your issues with alcohol, and your depression. Really, Rebecca, you have told him your story in your own way. He knows it, if he does inquire about your past, let him feel comfortable asking questions; if he perceives you are hiding something, and being evasive, you will better your chances of losing him. Both of you will need to bring closure with honesty. Let him know you are comfortable and understanding of any questions. Just avoid details and sidebars. Tim wants this to work just as much as you do. He is a good man."

"Roland, can I impose on you, by having Tim talk with you, as well?

"If he feels the need to."

"Roland, I know I am asking a lot of you at times, and place you in conflict with your soul. Unlike yourself, I am an atheist, and do not believe in a soul or any judgment day. I know this is what you believe, and will make sacrifices for your eternal rewards. My rewards are what I can touch, I need a tangible reality. Why is the truth so important to you, Roland? You yourself have said your morality, ethics and honesty never served you well. You insist you are not a martyr, yet you have paid a terrible personal loss on account of it."

"Rebecca, lies can never correct our human frailties. We use them only to hide behind, only to have them expose us for what we truly are. As children we are taught how to tell the truth, though we do not have to be instructed on how to lie. It is better to rise above the profane mortals who attach themselves to the flesh, as they do to their lies. How many people place on their resumes they are consummate liars?"

"I am sorry, Roland, remember the time, a few years back, when Tim was out of town on a business trip, and I went to a bar, got drunk, met some guy and had sex with him in my car? I was so shit-faced. Then, when I was sobering up, and he left, I started feeling really guilty. Then I drove to your place, so I could get myself together, staying the rest of the weekend, just to keep myself out of more trouble."

"How could I forget, it killed my weekend plans."

"Well, Roland, I know you never went behind my back to tell Tim. I really appreciated your good judgment. I know this placed you in deep conflict with your soul, and with your divided loyalties. How did you reconcile this within you, while maintaining your friendship with Tim and me? I really believed you would never have anything to do with us again."

"Rebecca, I never reconciled it within myself; contradiction and hypocrisy are some of my fiercest adversaries. When Tim returned home, you greeted him with a peace of mind, knowing you would not be found out. When I see Tim, and look into his eyes, I see an honorable man looking into the eyes of a devil."

"Roland, you need not carry my cross, it is my burden to carry. If it gives you any consolation, remember you were the first person I came to, knowing I could trust you. Would you rather I stayed at the bar after my little indiscretion, to drink off my guilt, like Nancy? Only to get behind the wheel of my car and kill myself or some innocent person? Would you be happier today knowing your honesty and trust prevented me from seeking your intervention? It's OK for you to not forgive me for my indiscretions … it is not right for you not to forgive yourself for your valor."

"Roland, you have got to ease off on yourself! Don't you ever get tired of carrying those stone tablets etched with your commandments down your holier-than -thou mountain? Leave that to Moses … Roland, unlike yourself, I fight my demons with each thought of a new day. Unlike you, who can make them dance to your command. If you are a Magnus, a true alchemist, why can't you transmute me and release me of my demons, free me before I fall prey to my own trap? Talk to me in my language of the flesh, and not in your lofty language of whatever the fuck you practice. Roland, can you help me without judging me?"

"Rebecca, I have always been here for you. If I were judging you, I would not be helping you. All we must do each morning when we look ourselves in the mirror is to ask ourselves: Will I let my soul rule the flesh? Or have the flesh rule my soul? If we choose the latter, our flesh is the aroma that will draw our hungry demons. Rebecca, your desires are no different from most people. You need to realize that the holiest of men are not immune from the temptations and the pleasures of the flesh. For if they were they would not be saints, but rather sterile eunuchs. The whore and the saint share the same demons."

"O, Roland, spare me your fucking sermons … I'm an atheist … I don't believe in your God."

"This is your choice, Rebecca, though you believe in demons?"

"Demons are my gods, because they have power over me!"

"Rebecca, you need to take stock in yourself, and to look deep into your soul, and make peace with your pains inflicted upon you from an abusive father. Drinking you only puts your sorrows to sleep, though never kills the pain of the memory. You must gather all your courage from within, and cut yourself free from your father's strings that still control you like a puppet."

"I'm, sorry Roland, for going off at you again. You know how I really feel about you. Sometimes I just can't figure you out."

"Roland, I am going to miss you, who is going to look out for me in Oregon?" Hey, Roland, another toast to our friendship! Now I want to pick your existential and moralist brain even more. Let me pose this moral conundrum to you, Mr. Christian. Let's see how you can reason your way out of this one."

"Please, engage me."

"Roland, do you find me attractive?"

"Yes."

"Do you find me sexy?"

"Yes."

144

"When I shower at your place … do you appreciate my body in the nude?"

Of course, you are an attractive woman."

"If Tim left me, would you then believe it would not be wrong for us to have an affair?"

"Correct."

"Well, then, Roland, are you not now breaking one of your hollowed commandments? Thou shall not covet thy neighbor's wife?"

"For the sake of debate, you have already sinned just by desiring me, and if you persist in resisting me, you are then a hypocrite. Right, Roland?"

"Nice try, Rebecca, and I do appreciate your Socratic methodology, both on an existential and spiritual level. Though, it has a caveat, that being that the word 'covet' by definition is to desire wrongfully, inordinately, or without due regard for the rights of others. And, if I denied your beauty, I would be lying, i.e., bearing a false witness, which is also a mortal sin. Therefore, I am not guilty of telling a lie, which may be hurtful to you. As far as desire, my thoughts and love for you are genuine, with no hidden agendas, nor did I ever feel incomplete for not having made love to you. And, the fact you are married to a man who has all the trust in the world for me, I would also be guilty of lying by the sin of omission. Rebecca, I love you too much as a friend, to lose you as a lover."

"Roland, I know you are right, I love Tim, but I have trouble keeping my demons down. You are the Adept who knows better to feed your angels and starve your demons. But life is so unfair, Roland. Just look at our friendship, if it were not for you, who would take me to these highbrow gallery openings, jazz concerts, and Yo Yo Ma concerts? Tim, knows well enough this is not his lifestyle. He is a nuts-and-bolts guy. As I mature I am finding we have less and less in common. And, he is a terrible romantic. It is just so unfair."

"Rebecca, it is, but we have to find our peace, no matter how painful it is."

"Roland, how do you find your peace, in the whirlwind life you lead?"

"Rebecca, I made a decision early on in my life to choose the arduous path ... as my destiny. I have made peace with my choice."

"Well, Roland, I do hope you come visit us in Oregon. Promise?"

"I will follow my path as far as it will let me."

After Tim and Rebecca's farewell party at Picasso's Palette, I drove them to the airport and bid them farewell with all the fanfare and smiles of friendship. I knew it would be the last time I would ever see them. As Tim was unpacking the luggage, I had a few last moments with Rebecca.

"Hey, Roland, thanks for the journey. Well, if you ever get a knock on your door in the middle of the night, for sure it will be me ... who has just left Tim. Then, you will have to keep your promise."

She whispered in my ear, and gave me a big hug and kiss.

"Hey, Rebecca, now make me this promise. Take this sealed envelope, and open it on the date marked on the back – promise me."

"Is this one of your Talismans inside, Roland?"

"Rebecca, please, and promise me ... consider it a last request."

"What are you telling me, Roland?"

I gave her a big hug, and gentleman's kiss.

"Good bye Rebecca, soon we will both find our peace."

146

Tarmac, Talismans and Tantra

I received Candy's email, confirming her 5: 15 p.m. arrival time. Her late arrival afforded me time to address some last-minute errands, and business I needed to attend to. I made sure the loft would be fitted with flowers, incense and, of course, the Donovan CD. I went to meet some business friends and associates earlier in the day at Karen's Kitchen to hand out some checks. Then headed out to pick up my Stratocaster from Samuel's, the local luthier, then headed up to Poughkeepsie to have lunch with Beth at our favorite Sushi restaurant.

By the time I arrived, Beth was already seated at our favorite table. She was just as beautiful and sexy as Rebecca, and could pass as her twin – though a few years older. The only difference being, Beth was also a practitioner of the *Kama Sutra*, seeking a higher form of sexuality on a spiritual level – she understood the art, enabling us to reach a sacramental sexuality. Basically, Rebecca on sexual steroids. She was also very spiritual and well versed in many forms of holy writ.

"Hey, Roland, I arrived here a little early, so I ordered us some Sake to get us started. Not into that wrecked Absinthe like you and Rebecca. It's just not you. I thought I would catch up with you before you catch up with your student paramour. Hey, Roland, is that simple country girl into the *Kama Sutra*, or just straight missionary position?"

"Hey, Beth, a true gentleman never kisses and tells."

"Well, Roland, if she is coming to see you all the way from Idaho, and staying with you for the next week, this speaks for itself."

"Well, I am feeling a bit indifferent about our reunion. Candy said she wants to see me to redeem herself."

"Redeem herself for what, Roland? What could a smart and beautiful person possibly have done to require redeeming herself from? You mention how much you enjoyed her company, and how you miss her, yet you keep talking about this dark cloud over the relationship – though you never tell me the details."

"Hey, Beth, I promise I will tell you after our roundelay. I hope the matter will be resolved once and for all."

"So, Roland, are you going to introduce me to her? Would love to meet her. I am sure we would become good friends, and Roland, before I forget, when you say you don't kiss and tell, is this just for your women friends? When you talk to your guy friends, I mean do you do the guy talk thing? Do you share with them any details about me?"

"Hey Beth, of course! I tell them how we enjoy going to museums, art galleries, listen to classical music, and fine dining."

"O fuck you Roland, your friends must think of you as some kind of lame eunuch, and me being a desperate, frigid, and needy woman?"

"That is my intention, all my guy friends are married or in long-term monogamous relationships. If I reveal the details of our sexuality, they would begin to start cheating on their partners, or demand from their partners expectations of better sex. In any case, the next time we socialize with them, their women will hate you, as they watch their men drool over you."

"You're right, Roland. Do they share any of their sexual exploits with you?"

"Regretfully so."

"How so, Roland?"

"O – I pray for their poor wrecked starved souls. They reduce sexuality to the basest of levels. The profane have a difficult time understanding it."

"Do you ever talk to them about the *Kama Sutra* to try to help them enhance their sexuality?"

"They would never be able to comprehend it, their views and practices are still at the puberty level of strip clubs, pole dancers, centerfolds and porn. They have a limited understanding of sexuality. For me to attempt to enlighten them on a sacred sexuality would be akin to throwing pearls before swine. Imagine, grown adults, going to a strip club, watching women and men undress, under the tackiest of ambience, getting all aroused, knowing they can't touch the object of their unfulfilled desires. Look at the absurdity of it all, it's like getting people who have not eaten in days, taking them to a barbeque to watch and smell the food as it is being prepared, only to tell them they can't eat it. The profane love to torture themselves in their hell with their own fire and brimstone."

"Hey, Roland, good point. I get it, you will lose all your guy friends, though look at the bright side, all their wives would want to fuck you."

"A dreadful option, celibacy would be the better option. Beth, you know how easy it is to determine someone's level of sexuality."

"O, Roland, I have to hear this, pray tell!"

"The next time you are at a restaurant, watch what people order, and how they eat. If they select the lightest of foods with the most textures, aromas, and spices that challenge their sensations they are candidates for the *Kama Sutra*. Those who select the heaviest of meals, with the least texture and aromas are just interested in filling their stomachs – they have no life esthetics. For instance, in my younger days of seduction, I remember an affair where I was in bed with a rather beautiful woman. Her lovemaking was short just like her eating habits, she just wanted to fill her stomach as soon as possible. And, just wanted to fill her orifices as soon as possible. I counted the minutes till morning, just for her to leave. I felt no physical or spiritual satisfaction. For me it was a sexual hell, for the profane it was heaven worthy to be noted in one's journal."

"O, yes, Roland, for us we lose ourselves within ourselves, time has no jurisdiction over us, as we reach the highest heavens of our mutual spiritual organisms. Our senses come alive in the texture of each new caress and kiss, in fear the dawn will not tarry long."

"Yes, Beth, it is a sensuality that will reveal ourselves behind the eternal veil." "What does this mean, Roland? Why do you always leave me with these opened-ended mystery clues?"

"No mysteries, Beth, Just closing statements. Now, back to the flesh, let's order; I have to head out soon. What are you planning for the week?"

"I will just pack over the weekend, attend my Zen meditation class, and then head out to Oregon on Monday to help Tim and Rebecca settle in. I hope this works out for them, and gets Rebecca back on the wagon. I spoke with her the other day, she was kind and honest enough to tell me about the conversation she had with you before she left. Thanks for not doing anything with her behind my back, and Tim's."

"To be honest, it was not easy; you both have been blessed with an abundance of beauty."

"Sorry for the non sequitur, I have to ask you: I don't mean to pry, but when I stopped by your loft earlier today to pick up my guitar, I overheard an incoming call on your telephone; it was another call from Roseland Medical saying you have been bumped from the list? And to call back ASAP. What is this all about Roland?"

"Nothing to concern yourself with, Beth. Must have something to do with a donation of some sort."

"So, Roland, what are your plans with Candy? Rebecca tells me she has quite a good taste for expensive and sexy lingerie – is she one of those innocent-looking angelic country girls on the outside, hiding a demon's passion in her soul?"

"Our plans for this evening to go to Demitasse for dinner, stay for the blues show, then head to my place. Not sure what is in store for us for the rest of the week. Depends on what news she bears."

"Roland, maybe you got her pregnant and she is coming with your new child? I am sure your daughters will appreciate this. By the way, when was the last time you talked with your daughters? O – Roland, I will pick up the tab, and don't forget you promised me a weekend in New Hope, PA"

"Sure, Beth, just book it for the Thanksgiving weekend ... I have to run!"

At my loft, I caught up on my paperwork and returned all my business calls. As I sorted my mail I came across a few letters from the Roseland Medical Center. I filled out the forms, along with a check, to be sent out immediately. I also sent copies to my accountant and lawyers. Around 3-ish the cleaning lady left, allowing me time to shower and change for dinner. On my way out I received a call from my good friend Kathryn, who I have known since I was a teenager. She was a platonic friend, and we were each other's confidants. She also assisted me behind the lines with my stealth personal matters.

"Hi Kathryn, so glad to hear from you. I was planning to call you Monday to give you an update. I will also be mailing you a package with all the paperwork, arrangements, and instructions. ... I will drop it off at the post on my way out tonight. If you are free I can meet you for lunch sometime next week in Greenwich."

"Sounds good, Roland. If I have any questions with the paperwork I will call you. I will also get back to you with a day I can meet for lunch. I will also to try to find a place with a water view ... enjoy your dinner with Candy. Soon your work will be done, and you will no longer have to walk the arduous trail."

An Angel's Tempest

Candy emerged from the terminal with her luggage, looking radiant in her designer jeans, turtleneck and black letter jacket. She had not aged a day since I last saw her, though she had matured in how she carried herself: more confident and aware of her own identity, though never vain nor arrogant. Her thick blond hair fell upon her shoulders like a waterfall, her aviator sunglasses and pointed knee-high boots made her very chic. She was no longer the simple country girl in my Economics class. I pulled up in front of her as I lowered the passenger window.

"Hello, Candy, how was your flight, I will help you with your luggage."

As I got out of the car, she walked over to greet me with a big smile, hug and kiss.

"Hi, Roland, so glad to see you, I hope all is well."

"Candy, you are radiant as ever."

"Roland, we have some time, so let's head to your place, and I can freshen up first, and finally put your moral and pious concerns aside, once and for all. Roland, I love you, but you need to stop looking for an absolution from your imagined sin."

"This would offer me peace of mind in light of my present circumstances."

"Roland, for a deep existential thinker, on a spiritual quest – an Adept of the Great Work – you are stuck in the shallow waters of your own self-righteousness."

"Well, Candy, I pray, you have come today with news that corrects the injustice inflicted on me with your parting note."

"Roland, I am humbled by your rigid standards, and support them. This is why I have these feelings for you, and want to be a part of your Great Work. But you are contradicting yourself. You yourself have written in one of your books on moral philosophy that it is the laws of the soul that should never be transgressed, which trump arbitrary and capricious temporal laws. Yet now you place a dated piece of dead paper drafted by a temporal hand above the law of the soul, in total disregard for the victim. Do you need your self- pity and pride to be above the pain of the victim, who you rescued? Roland, I am here to bring good news for both of us."

"Candy, so where is the good news?"

"I have it in my suitcase. I will share it with you when we get to the loft."

"Roland, allow me a few minutes to freshen up, we have time to talk before we head out for dinner. I see you have your Stratocaster ready to go."

"I will pour some wine as you freshen up."

"We will need it, Roland … thanks!"

"Roland, you need to be open-minded about this, OK?"

"Sure. Candy, you know from my class the rules of the debate: no emotion and stick to the facts, no non-sequiturs."

"O, Roland, for fucking sakes, this is a talk about our emotions and future, not a sterile debate on theoretical social economics. This is not an immutable mathematical equation … remember, you are the seeking spiritual pilgrim, an Adept of the Inner Light. Please, invoke your talismans of Divine Wisdom upon our reunion. Please!"

"Candy, I promise; there are more days behind me than there are before me. We will need to cleanse these dark spots from our souls."

"Roland, there are no dark spots on our souls. You have not

sinned, and I am not an adulteress. And, since when have you added drama and theatrics to your conversations? For heaven's sake, you are only 53 years old, … not 80!"

"Candy, you know very well my views on adultery. You must understand where I am coming from … I never wanted to be labeled a hypocrite – especially when it comes to having an affair with a married woman."

"Roland, now stop it, you are no more a hypocrite than I am adulterous!"

"Candy, how can you say this? When we made love you told me you were divorced. Then you leave a letter behind, a confession of sorts, stating that the divorce was rejected in Florida, since it needed to be filed in New York State. So you were legally married, making me guilty of having an affair with a married woman."

"Damn you, Roland, wake up, and stop languishing in your fool's paradise of guilt. You forget you are also my mentor! Do I have to remind you of your moral lessons? Did you not state, these are your words – 'Even the peacemaker must pick up the sword to defend a woman's honor?' Aren't you entitled to the awards of your chivalry? You defended me, and gave me hope, you gave me the courage to stand up against that bully husband of mine! And, besides, never question my morality, Roland! I was a virgin, up until the wedding night of my marriage. I am a good Methodist woman. And, I have only had sex with two men in my life! My ex-husband and you! Are you implying I have made two poor choices in selecting my men? And besides, Roland! How many women have you fucked in the last year? And, if I had whispered in your ear as we were lying naked in our embraces that I was still technically married, would you have stopped? Besides, Roland, I thought you saintly types practice celibacy. You use your 'holy" hands to clasp in prayer, and to hold my breasts in heated passions."

"Alright, Candy, your questions are true and spoken with passion. Now please share with me your good news, I would imagine this would change my perspective on this situation."

"As promised in the letter I left you, all would be resolved to our favor. And, to provide you with even more certainty about me having any contact or feelings about my ex-husband. In my suitcase I have the certificate of divorce, and my ex-husband's death certificate."

"A death certificate?"

"Well, Roland, I am beginning to believe there is something to this synchronicity you speak of, and the universal laws of justice. My ex-husband died of an overdose while awaiting trial. He did not have the time, nor the sense, to review his will, failing to realize in his inebriated states he had left me as his sole beneficiary. Maybe that purification ritual you performed before we made love caught the attention of heavenly justice."

"This more than places my soul at ease. We have been favored and blessed with divine justice."

"Roland, it gets better than this! My ex-husband fell into a deep depression after his arrest, after he realized he was nothing but a pawn in a chess game being played out between the University and HAL. An investigative reporter exposed to the press a conspiracy masterminded by the University and HAL, and named my ex-husband as a co-conspirator. The University and HAL are under investigation by the Attorney General's office, and have indicted your 'friends,' even Dean Ganelon, as well as the Bishop."

"Roland, I am sure this is music to your ears, since you suspected this all along. The Dean of the Computer Science department used his daughter as a whore, who worked at HAL and was on the grant committee. She fell for my ex-husband's physical and well-endowed anatomy and sexuality, along with all his S&M and kinky fetishes – unknown to me. As long as he was under her spell, she approved generous grants to the University. Through a number of rather inventive accounting practices, the deans, along with the Bishop, were the recipients of the lion's share of the money. When the investigation was launched by the AG's office, they needed a sacrificial lamb in an attempt to throw off the investigation. You are named in the AG's suit, as one of the plaintiffs. I would recommend you contact my attorney, Mr. Lovetti. You see, Roland, you have been redeemed for your morality, and imagined illicit affair."

Do You Believe in Magic?

"Roland, please excuse me while I get ready for our reunion dinner at Demitasse. I believe I left a few of my articles of clothing here, where may I find them?"

"Pretty much where you left them."

Candy then went upstairs to unpack. Soon she emerged from the bedroom loft, wrapped in a towel, holding all her toiletries. I had turned on the water jets for her in the interim. She dropped her towel entered the shower, enjoying the sensations of the multiple water jets. She lathered herself up, washed her hair with the most graceful motions. Grabbing her towel she wrapped it around her head like a turban and walked over to the kitchen island to pour herself another glass of wine. "Roland, I won't be long, just turn on some soft music."

She then ascended the loft stairwell with confident nudity.

"Ready, Roland, how do I look?"

She was wearing the same outfit that she had left here, a pleasant memory of our first evening of intimacy.

"Stunning, as always, Candy!"

I picked up my Stratocaster with my left hand, and held her hand with my right. Like our first dinner at Demitasse, it was a beautiful autumn evening, full of magical memories. I loaded my Stratocaster into my new SUV, and headed up to Poughkeepsie.

"Candy, how long are you planning to stay?"

"Well, Roland, this depends on what happens this evening. I would like to stay as long as possible, and to see where we can take this relationship. Do you have any thoughts about this, as well as how you feel about me? Do you love me Roland?"

"More then you will know. I missed you, Candy, over this past year. I have never felt this way about a woman before."

"Roland, are you ready to give up your lover, Beth, for me?"

"Yes, and without reservation, Candy."

"Roland, I am moved, I was expecting some hesitation, or I-will-think-about-it answer. I am pleasantly surprised about your ease with making this commitment. What changed in your life?"

"Candy you are well aware I am 53 years old, a full generation apart.

"Roland, please, why the drama and melancholy?"

"Are you aware of the realities of this type of relationship?"

"Roland, I am sure, but please tell me why the change of heart. What changed since last year?"

"Well, Candy, a few days ago I was in a deep meditation and ritual, using my third eye to seek guidance as to how to proceed with my life."

"Roland, please … keep going what did you see?"

"I was in this deep trance brought on by a Coptic Christian meditation. I saw you in a white angelic gown, casting light that emanated from your womb into a dark abyss. You were smiling, to the point of bliss. You then looked at me with true radiant eyes summoning me to you. You held a tall unlit candle in your hand. You told me to light the candle. As I did, gold wax dripped down the shaft, until there was nothing left but a small residue of gold. You next placed your right hand on my heart. As you retracted your soft hand stained with the blood from your heart, you mixed the blood with the gold residue. Next you placed this mixture in the palm of your left hand. With your right hand you scribed one Rosicrucian cross upon the chest on my white tunic. Next you scribed another Rosicrucian cross across the breast of your tunic. Then you took what was left of the residue and cast in on the ground before you. Soon a tree of Divine Wisdom grew out of the earth. As it grew bigger the huge branches formed into alabaster classrooms, lit by exotic gems. In the center of the tree trunk, I saw a majestic door open wide, revealing a young boy with golden hair that radiated divine knowledge. Then both of you looked in my direction looking upon a big bonfire of knowledge, emitting light into the darkness."

"Roland, what does this mean? Do you know how to interpret this vision? What is it telling you? What kind of omen is this?"

"Candy, if you commit to this relationship, you will be asked to walk the arduous path with me. Are you ready to take on this journey?"

"What will it require of me, Roland? Do you know?

"Candy, we will talk later when our flesh and soul are united as one, only then will you truly understand."

As we entered the open courtyard, a waiter escorted us to our favorite table. It was set with the finest of linen, silverware and crystal. The waiter seated us, handing us the wine list.

"Candy, are you up to sampling a little Absinthe? This is one of the few places in the Hudson valley that actually knows how to properly prepare it. Believe me, Candy, this will be a very special evening for both of us. Just smell the fresh autumn air, look up at the full moon, feel the soft rustle of the leaves, listen to your heart, and fill all your senses with love and joy. Now what about the Absinthe?"

"Sure, I am up to it," she said, as her smile radiated as in my vision.

"Waiter, two Absinthes please, prepared as usual. Candy, tonight I have a few special surprises for you. I am having my band Cygnus Ollor perform for us tonight, and will sit in on a few songs to be dedicated to you. As expected, a blues set, with my cover of *Boom Boom Boom*."

"Roland? Doesn't *cygnus ollor* mean the swan song? Roland, what are you trying to say? Should I be concerned?"

"Candy, no please, did you know that Swans mate for life? And, the legend goes, the mute swan sings before its death. Candy, we all have a swan song, and like swans we have a life-long mate to sing it to. Do you feel the magic in the air tonight? We will be blessed with a new mission and life, and will plant the seeds for a better tomorrow. The heavens look down on us tonight with favor."

"Roland, when you first saw me, did you know this would be the outcome?"

"Candy, when I first set eyes on you, I felt an infinity I could not comprehend."

"Maybe we were lovers and mystics in a previous life."

"Candy, tell me, why did you approach me for help, and not any of your other professors?"

"Roland, maybe it was synchronicity. Or, maybe it was magic."

I finished my blues set, then turned the remainder of the show back to the band, so I could spend the rest of the evening dancing with Candy. We held each other tight, then I whispered in her hear to promise to never divulge the secret I was going to share with her.

"I promise Roland ... I understand. But why? Why now? Why you? Why me? The blessing is not worth the pain."

"Candy, it is not an option, only my fate and your destiny now."

"Roland, I understand ... Yes, to both questions. What is next, Roland?"

I whispered in her ear, then we danced past midnight oblivious to the mortal world.

The Mysteries of Eulis

"Roland, why in heaven's name are you taking this on?"

"Candy, I have no choice in the matter, it must be completed, and it will be my blessing to complete my work using Christian Tantrism as the vehicle to liberate my soul, and to use the toils of my flesh to bring happiness to others. It is only through you I will be able to complete the Great Work. Like the Mahayana Buddhists, true Christian Gnostics take unto themselves the suffering of others to give happiness to others. We strive to transform others' suffering into happiness, chiefly through spiritual means, rituals and good intentions. Tonight, we will not just be lovers, but will be wed spiritually as our flesh and souls become one. I will plant the seeds for the earthly mission of the Great Work, and for our eternal future. Our flesh will surrender its identity to the profane by dawn, and we will only be recognized by works of our souls. We will be outliers and outcasts among the profane who seek the ignorance of the herd. They travel in numbers lost to their true identity."

"Roland, if you are a true Adept and a member of the Illuminati, why do you still go to Catholic Confession? And convert to Mormonism?"

"Gnostic Christians need to find a local established faith just for the purpose of having a place to pray, and most importantly, to blend in. We have always been persecuted, by the small minds of the practicing profane. We all have suffered dearly in our past lives for our true faith. Wherever we go, we keep our identity silent, we never seek converts, and we just set a higher example for humanity to follow. Candy, would you have approached me if I told you I was a practicing Adept?"

Candy then went upstairs to get ready, as I prepared the chamber for our ritual. She descended the stairs wearing her white ritual garment, her golden hair falling upon her shoulders, her blue eyes shined like sapphires. As she smiled her aura glowed. I turned on the shower, then she dropped her garment revealing her beautiful body. I soon joined her as we washed each other as we prepared ourselves for each other. We touched each other's bodies with affection, saving our passions for later, as we teased and tantalized our five senses of sight and sound, of touch and taste, and smell. The *Kama Sutra* teaches that lovemaking is not limited to intercourse, but real sex begins long before arousal and continues on as lovers meditate and read poetry after having united their souls. We nibbled and nuzzled each other as we lightly kissed and caressed. We then walked to the sanctuary. The Swarnanabba says a man should always press upon the points of a woman on which she turns an eye. I toweled her off, as I slowly moved down between her legs rubbing and arousing her gently.

I next scribed a circle on the floor around the ritual chamber, as I recited the holy words to consecrate our union, of our sacramentum magum:

Copula canalis, vaga inter illos, non est peccatum, sed sacramentum magnum ... Sacrum Scripturam ita interpretantu, ot omnia carnali senu accipiant.

I then escorted Candy to the center of the circle, as I began walking three times around the circle, circling to the left, to remove all unwanted negative energies and demons. I then walked three circles to the right, chanting as I looked at the center of the circle. We next performed our Heart Salutation as we faced each other in the center of our magic circle. As we stood about eighteen inches apart, we brought our hands together in the front of our chests pressed lightly together. We then bowed bending slowly forward from the waist, until our foreheads touched, then slowly straightening ourselves back into an upright position.

I then offered up my invocations of protection, and procreation:

> *Christ, I adjure you, O lord, almighty, first begotten, self-begotten, as well as all-seeing are you, and Yao, Sabao, Brinthao: Keep me as a son, protect me from every evil spirit, and subject to me every spirit of impure, destroying demons – on the earth, under the earth, of the water and of the land – and every phantom. Christ.*
>
> *Almighty master, Lord, O god, since from the beginning you have created humankind in your likeness and in your image, you also have honored my striving for childbirth. You said to our mother Sarah, 'At this time in a year a son will be born to you.' Thus also now, look, I invoke you, who is seated upon the cherubim, that you listen to my request today – me, Roland, son of Raymond over the chalice of wine that is in my hand, so that Candice, daughter of Magdalene, you may favor her with a human seed. And, Lord, who listens to everyone who calls upon you, Adoni Elon Sabaoth, God of Gods and Lord of Lords, and through this chalice let her be released through redeeming love … I adjure you by your great name and the suffering you experienced upon the cross: You must bring to pass the words … that have been spoken over this chalice in my hand.*

To ward off incubi and succubae, and to gain favor of the invisible forces we burned white and black benzoin perfumes, elemi resin, aloe wood, coriander and myrrh. For an added measure we burned some Boswellia serrata. With the ritual complete, I took Candy's hand and walked her over to the bed, with sheets prepared with a mixture of spring water and neroli oil. She removed her white ritual gown and laid on her stomach. I massaged her arms with mint, her jaws and breasts with palm oil, her neck and knees with rose essence. A pomade from marjoram was placed in her hair. I then gently massaged her back with sandal oil. I then rubbed her back and buttocks with both hands, moving down her legs. Candy then lifted her feet to be massaged. Next I removed my robe, then laid down in bed on my back, as Candy got up to sit astride me to message my chest in musk oil. Next we kissed each other's nape of the neck, forehead, eyes, cheeks, throat, the bosom, the breasts, the lips and the interior of the mouth.

Next I sucked Candy's breast and nipples; they were pearls never to be thrown before dogs. I then inserted my hand within her to stoke the Kundalini fire within her.

"My beloved put his hand by the hole in the door,
and my innermost part shivered"
Solomon 5:4

"I rose up to open to my beloved,
and my hands were dripped with myrrh,
and my fingers with sweet smelling myrrh,
upon the handles of the lock"
Solomon 5:5

To activate the first chakra wave, Candy sat before me with her legs crossed in a half lotus position, as I faced her with my legs spread. I next placed my left hand on her "mound of Venus"

(Muladhara chakra) while I placed my right hand on her hara chakra (below the naval) with a circular motion, slowly moving up all her chakras until I reached the crown chakra. Candy moved to the rhythm of each chakra.

Next, Candy, sat behind me performing the first chakra wave on me. Then I approached her breasts, making spiral movements around them, slowly decreasing the radius until I reached her nipples.... To increase my energy I rubbed my thumbs and index fingers together to generate more chi. Then I touched her nipples by rolling them between my two heated fingers. I repeated this movement around her breasts with my tongue, to arouse Candy's female sexual energy. As our sexual energies were aroused, I seated Candy next to me on cushions with her legs spread, then began to excite her yoni with a two-finger basic stroke, a double stroke, a rooted stroke, then a three-finger tickle stoke and finally direct stimulation.

I continued on with my White Magic of Love ritual as I followed her Yin meridian to her conception vessel as I traveled up from her Gate of Life and Death in her base chakra, kissing her naval, solar plexus, heart center, then her throat to combine our love and sex energies, yin and yang, and fire and water elements.

Candy then rolled me on my back to perform the nine-flower massage beginning with my chest to harmonize our hearts and minds; then she massaged the underswell of my chest; moving down to the third flower to warm my ribs to soften anxiety and indecision; she softly moved down to my solar plexus to digest our love; moving down to my naval to awaken my sensuality; next she moved her fingers to my Sea of Chi, the male sexual center, and the most potent male arousal point that connects with the essence of the feminine reproductive cycle; as she moved her way down to heaven she softly touched and stroked my lower abdomen; then finally she presented her eighth and ninth flowers as she slowly and softly caressed my Gate of Life and Death, taking us to heaven. We repeated our heavenly descents on each other substituting our fingers with or tongues to heighten the senses of our meridians.

We laid side by side facing each other in an embrace as I placed my leg between her legs to stimulate her clitoris with my thigh. We then engaged in our first position of congress, as Candy laid on her back, she pressed her two feet against my chest, then she placed her legs around my neck, as we then explored the many ways of the *Kama Sutra*.

We prolonged our lovemaking until dawn, as she exchanged her keemlin sexual fluids with my geehr sexual fluids. When combined in the body, they create around the entwined couple an aura – the Ethylle – which has an irresistible power of attraction on entities from the spirit world. A true Adept knows the universe is bathed in the Aeth, which contains the celestial hierarchies as known by the Holy Scriptures; the angels, seraphs, arsaphs; and all the Potentialities in their pure state. It is in these spiritual spheres that the germs of all knowledge and power reside. When a man and woman consummate their true love for one another, these soul-seeds, germs of knowledge and their magic powers, find lodgment in their souls and the mystic's door opens and shuts for them. For the Adept to channel this heavenly magic upon himself, his partner must not be a married woman, prostitute or a child. As the light of dawn cast its first rays upon our naked bodies, we showered together as we embraced and made love again, Varikrida style – the water game.

We then went back to lay on our ritual bed to hug and caress, as I read her my poems of love. Candy then whispered, "Roland, how long?"

"Candy, we will marry within the month. We don't have much time to make arrangements, I will set the date as October 23rd."

Candy then turned to me with a broken smile, "I now understand Roland."

I placed my hand on her stomach, "Now Candy, let's get moving, you have a wedding dress to pick out, and I have some unfinished business to address."

Sanctuary

"Hello, Kathryn, I hope you and the family are doing well. I will need for you to attend my gallery auction this month to handle the closing of the accounts. I also have a rather long to-do list for you, not to mention helping me plan my wedding."

"Wedding, Roland, when did this come about, especially in light of your recent news? Who is the woman? Anyone I know? Sorry, Roland, I am happy for you, it is just that it comes as such a surprise at this time of your life."

"Kathryn, I will introduce you to my bride before the wedding. In the meantime, I will need for you to make arrangements to rent out a church, send out invitations and book the reception for October 23rd."

"Why, Roland, that's only weeks away! Well, I have us booked for dinner on Thursday in Greenwich, at your favorite spot at 7. You can fill me in with the details then,"

"O, before I forget, you have to book me a round-trip flight to Paris next week."

"Roland, what is going on, how am I going to pull this off in only a few weeks?"

"Sorry, Kathryn, I will have Candice help you, my bride-to-be has all the details and knows what has to be done."

"Remember the silence referring to time."

"Of course, Roland. See you Thursday."

"Roland, Lovetti's office called with the settlement number; regarding the class action suit, the University agreed to your terms. Also, your artwork is being shipped and will arrive next week, with a staff to set it up for the exhibition. The appraiser will be arriving on the day of the opening. Also, I confirmed your flight, and the car service to take you to Montsegur, in the Languedoc. I booked you a room, and confirmed the architect Peire Autier will meet you there at the *prat dels cremats* (fields of the burned), and Guillaume Belibaste with the Bonhommes (Good Christians) will take you on a tour of the Pays Cathare."

"Thanks, Kathryn."

"O, Roland! How could I forget, the international mover called to confirm the move date to pack and transport your library – minus the books as requested – to the new library at Montsegur castle."

"Candy, the seamstress will be arriving around 2 to work on your gowns. We can pick up our wedding license on Friday. I secured the Chapel of the Martyrs on the Hudson for the service, booked all the rooms at the Hudson Bay Hotel for our out-of-town guests. The caterer will supply the tent, and all the trimmings. We need to keep the guest list down to 100 of our closest friends and family. I also made arrangements to have car service pick up all the guests arriving at the airport."

"O, Roland, before I forget, I received a call confirming that two Cathar Bishops will perform the ceremony, along with a few Prefecti. Also, Dr. Kraft from the Roseland Medical Center will be joining you on your flight and tour of the Pays Cathare. He will also attend the wedding as the Grand Master representing the Grand Lodge of the Illuminati and Rosicrucians."

The loft was active with phone calls and visitors.

"Roland, Kathryn is on the line, says it's important."

"Roland, sorry to bother you, just received a call from your real estate attorney, your loft has been sold, with a closing date of November 15th. All funds will be deposited in the Alexandria trust. And, your literary agent called, confirming two publishers are bidding on your manuscripts, and will have the deals wrapped up by the time you return from the Languedoc."

"Roland, lets confirm the guest list this evening, so we can get the invitations out tomorrow."

"Should not be a problem."

"Candy, who will be attending from your family? Your parents are in no condition to travel."

"True, my sisters are their caretakers now, so they will not be able to attend, and you know my brothers are overprotective, and against the wedding."

"Who is going to give you away, and who will be your bridesmaid?"

"Roland, I will have one of the Prefecti from the Languedoc walk me down as a proxy for my father. This should be fitting for the occasion."

"What about your bridesmaid? Who do you plan to select since your sisters are unable to attend?"

"Roland, I do not have any lady friends here, can you suggest someone? Someone who truly understands you; this is not your typical wedding."

"Well, I can only suggest someone, you can make the decision after you meet her."

"Who do you have in mind?"

"The only person that comes to mind is Beth, I have known her for a while, and I have shared our story with her. I have already called her and told her of our wedding plans."

"Well Roland, how did she take it, you are rather close."

"Surprised, of course, and happy for us. She does not know the whole picture, but soon will. I am going to meet her for coffee at 2 across the street at the café, to tell her our plans, then I will send her up to meet with you. She may play a larger role in this, and may one day be your best friend. After I send her up, I have to meet with my accountant, then the caterer. Do you have a preference for dinner? When I return we could head out to a quiet place."

"Roland, you need to slow down, I will make something for dinner, then we can go over the final plans. We need to wrap this up since you will be leaving for France next week to take care of business."

"Yes, I agree, there is much that needs to be done to ensure the success of the Great Work."

Beth was already at the table when I arrived, and had ordered us the usual. She was her usual self, smiling, very upbeat, and a bit confused.

"So Roland, so what the fuck is this, I just saw you a few days ago, and you were talking about this reunion of sorts with mixed emotions, and now you tell me you are going to marry her in a few weeks. I am really happy for you, not the least bit bitter, just really confused. I called Rebecca and Tim, and they are as confused and they are concerned."

Well, I hope you invited them to the wedding – all their expenses will be paid."

Roland, are you going through a mid-life crisis? Or has all that Absinthe made you mad? What gives? You are going to invite me, aren't you?"

"Of course I am going to invite you, and better yet, Candice is considering you as her maid of honor."

"Roland, you must be fucking crazy ... did one of your rituals go astray?"

"Beth, we are the best of friends, and former lovers, and besides, in a few hours you will know who we really are."

"O, fuck, Roland, how in heaven's name did we ever cross paths? How in hell is this going to work?"

"Well, Beth, I did tell Candice all about you, and us, and she does not have a problem with it. She is at the loft and would like to meet you to discuss the wedding. Will you go see her after we head out? I know you will bond well with her."

"Sure, Roland, I would not miss it for the world. You know, just when I think I have figured you out, you do something that really fucks with my head. Are there any other mysteries you are holding from me?"

"O, Beth, for sure, this is just the tip of the iceberg. More will be revealed soon."

"Roland, I can only imagine."

"Well, if you can, look after Candice for me while I am in France next week on business."

"Roland, what the fuck is going on? What the hell is in France; you never mentioned this to me in the past. What business dealing do you have in France? Well, Roland, I am glad you are making me a part of your special day. Sure, I will head up and talk with her."

"Thanks, Beth, I will take care of you for all your kindness and friendship, for sure it will be eternal bliss. Now help Candice pick out her gown, and yours as well."

"Roland, you sure you are not withholding something from me? You just don't seem right."

"All is good, Beth, believe me."

"O, Roland, only heaven knows, I guess."

"Right, Beth! I look forward to having you assist us in our wedding plans. Candice can use the help, and make a new true friend."

"Roland, where are you guys going on your honeymoon?"

"We are just staying in town."

"Roland, I just can't figure you out. You must be a genius or a madman!"

"Well, time will tell. Well got to run. I will most likely see you at the loft when I return from my meetings."

"Roland, what is it that makes you so different? And so hard to understand? You are always searching for something higher and unknown, your head is always in the the fucking clouds. What is it Roland?"

"Beth, my sanctuary is what I seek, and I have found it; Candice is the vessel that will take me to my long-sought-after sanctuary."

"O, Roland, I will see you later. Do you talk to Candice this way? Hell, I thought for a while that I was the only person who truly understood you, and knew who you are. Now I am not sure if I ever really knew you for who you really are. Roland, talk to me, please, explain to me who you really are. Roland, do you love me, have you ever loved me?"

"Beth, I loved you more than I could convey with my words, poems, and flesh; but, it is a love from my soul, the agape that I love you. In a short time you will know what this means. It is our synchronicity. We are part of the eternal river following with the continuum of time. To travel back to the land of whence we came. I ask you to take this journey with us."

"O, Roland, there you go again speaking in these riddles and mysteries. Why?"

"Beth, there are no riddles or mysteries, they are only the truths we fear to find."

The Alchemical Wedding

October 23, 1999

It was a beautiful cool autumn day, sunny, clear with a cool breeze. I stood at the chapel door gazing into the beautiful Hudson River. The sun glistened upon the river's calm blue waters. The river whispered my name, and a chill of peace overcame my soul. I no longer could see the arduous path before, only the eternity of Old Man River as I gazed to the east. By now a number of the Prefecti had arrived along with many of the Credentes. I walked up to the altar, kneeled, and said a few prayers before Bishop Fournier along with his two assistants the filius major, and the filius minor. The string quartet arrived and began to set up along with the hurdy-gurdy player. Dr. Kraft was in attendance along with a few of the Illuminati. The small chapel was now filled with friends, and my few remaining relatives.

We left the chapel doors open to let in more light and to feel the cool October breeze. I was now standing at the altar with my best man, Eric, my spiritual advisor, as the Hurdy Gurdy player started playing the Hersie de Cathars. Next Rebecca walked down the aisle as the Bridesmaid, followed by Beth as the maid of honor, both wearing a simple white gown holding a bouquet of fresh flowers just flown in from the Languedoc. The usher then seated the few remaining guests. Beth looked at me with an unfamiliar stare, as her eyes welled up with tears, failing in her attempts to smile. She whispered to me in low tones as she grabbed my hand.

"Roland, I am sorry. I have mixed feelings of joy and sorrow. Candice has shared your story, I now understand you, Roland."

She held my hand tight.

"Rest assured Dr. Roland Berengiere, my tears are those of joy, for Candice and I were visited by Sophia last evening while in our meditations. Your work was not done in vain, the heavens have not abandoned you, Roland. We are all one now as Bonhommes wedded for all eternity."

Rebecca turned to me, smiled, gave me a kiss, and then said, "Roland, you have purged me of my demons, I now believe, I am now one of the Bonhommes. Tim sends his love. Your note is now in my heart."

The string quartet stated to play as Candy was escorted down the aisle with one of the Prefecti, acting as proxy for her father. Candice was wearing a simple hooded gown, also holding a bouquet of flowers from the Languedoc. She took her place at my side. Eric then smiled at me, as he tried to hold back the tears. Bishop Fournier consecrated the marriage. Candice then pulled her hood down, as we performed our kiss of consecration. She looked beautiful, with her golden locks falling upon her shoulders, and with the fragrance of the fresh flowers she had tucked in her hair. Eric and Beth gave each other a hug and a kiss as we exited the chapel followed by all the guests who joined us at our tented reception party held next to the chapel, on the shore of the Hudson.

Candice and I danced for the first time as husband wife to the Cathar song *Des Oge mais*. We all danced into the night, around a bonfire pit next to the shore. As the party concluded, Candice and I stood by the ashen bonfire pit to collect some of the ashes. We were joined by the Bishop, The Grand Master, along with Eric, Beth and Rebecca. We stared into the pit, in a reverie, when the Bishop spoke.

"Soon a new light will resurrect itself from the ashes of dawn. Roland, you have marked you days well before God and man. And, have walked this promised land of errors with wisdom and fortitude. Blessings on your new journey."

Canδice Berengiere
(Postscript)

JOURNAL ENTRY:
OCTOBER 23, 2055

I was awakened by that mystical October breeze that warmed my soul and kindled my fond memories of Roland. I walked over to my window to take one final look at the majestic view of the Languedoc, along with the chapel, library and the school of Alexandria, now built high upon the ruins of Montsegur, and the meditation garden located on the grounds of the prat dels cremats. I had my nurse attendant call for my son, Alexandre, now 65, and my granddaughter, Sophia, to pass on Roland's original manuscripts of *the Rituals Cathare de Lyons,* and the *Liber de duobus principiis,* dating back to the date of the massacre of Montsegur, on March 15, 1244, perpetuated by the crusaders under orders by Pope Innocent III. I also passed on Roland's necklace Talisman he gave me on our wedding night. Even the knights Templar could not sway their fellow crusaders to end their war and genocide against the Cathars.

I so vividly remember our wedding night as we left our reception to go to Roland's loft for the last time. By the time we arrived Beth and Rebecca had set up our bed with satin sheets prepared with spring and rose water and neroli oil. Roland was fatigued and his skin was jaundiced; he put on a good front for all in attendance. His liver was in the final stages of failure, and no suitable donors for a transplant were to be found. We both knew his time was short. Roland was now too weak to perform the ritual of conception. I walked Roland over to the shower to help him undress, then joined him as we showered together to purify our flesh and souls for our evening lovemaking. The shower invigorated Roland as we toweled each other off to explore our sacred places, as we offered our final soft and tender kisses to each all over our bodies.

Roland's flesh was failing him, and his soul was now preparing to leave his body for his journey up the sacred river. To help him maintain his soul's energy, and spirit, I held his hand, and walked him to the center of our chamber. Roland had taught me well the rituals and rules of Gnostic magic, as I then started the consecration of the blessed circle. I spoke those words with the power of love:

Copula canalis, vaga inter illos, non est peccatum, sed sacramentum magnum ... Sacrum Scripturam ita interpretantu, ot omnia carnali senu accipiant.

I then escorted Roland to the center of the circle, as I began walking three times around the circle, circling to the left, to remove all unwanted negative energies and demons. I then walked three circles to the right, chanting as I looked at the center of the circle. We next performed our Heart Salutation as we faced each other in the center of our magic circle. As we stood about eighteen inches apart, we brought our hands together in the front of our chests pressed lightly together. We then bowed bending slowly forward from the waist, until our foreheads touched, then slowly straightening ourselves back into an upright position.

To ward off incubi and succubae, and to gain favor of the

invisible forces, we burned white and black benzoin perfumes, elemi resin, aloe wood, coriander, and myrrh. For an added measure we burned some Boswellia serrata. With the ritual complete I took Roland's hand and walked him over to the bed, and laid him on his stomach. I massaged his body with musk oil, mint and palm oil. I placed a pomade made from marjoram in my hair, then ran my fingers through Roland's hair. I then rubbed his back and buttocks with both hands, moving down his legs. We laid next to each other looking into each other's eyes, as we smiled and whispered our fantasies to each other. I then straddled him so we could each enjoy our nectars of our love, as my mouth caressed his lingam, and his tongue my yoni, we engaged in the many varieties of this soixante-neuf, known as the Kakila in the Indian tradition. I turned on my back, inviting Roland to take me in the Ekabandha position. The *Kama Sutra* teaches all its aspirants to prolong the pleasure of lovemaking by regulating our rhythms and breathing with slow deep breaths.

Roland then sat up in bed, as I sat upon his lap, and wrapped my legs around his waist, to enjoy all the pleasures of the Kirtibandha. We then went on and on exploring many of the sacred positions and mysteries of the *Kama Sutra*, far too numerous for my final entry. We then went to shower ourselves. As I changed the bedding, to prepare it for the next ritual Roland went to his office, returning with a packet containing, among others, instructions his final will and testament for me to execute.

Sensing the pain he was in, I placed him in bed, then called the Bishop, the Grand Master, and Beth, now a Bonhommes, to come over to give Roland his Consolamentum. I opened the drapes and the window so Roland could see the mystical river that was now calling him home. By now I even began to hear those whispering angelic voices telling Roland, he will no longer walk the arduous path. I sat next to him holding his hand, as he slipped in and out of consciousness. The Bishop and Grand Master arrived, along with Beth, and a few Bonhommes to perform the Consolamentum. Now Roland shunned food and water to speed up his death. He passed quietly and graciously within a few minutes, never having to suffer long during the endura.

I executed his last will and testament as requested. He was cremated having his ashes placed in three urns. His service was held at the Chapel of the Martyrs three days after our wedding, with all the wedding guests in attendance. As the guests started to arrive, Roland's attorney was present holding a brief case, and watching as friends came to pay their last respects. He walked over to me, and then asked me to join him inside the chapel. Once inside, he opened the briefcase, and handed me a small jewelry box, then asked me to open it in front of him. Inside was a glass cross filled with a pinkish red fluid attached to a necklace of solid gold, with pearls. Inside the box was a note from Roland that read:

My Beloved Candice,
Attached in my Rosy Cross I will no longer have to wear. It is filled with my blood, sweat and tears. Wear it at all times, to protect you as you now walk the arduous path. Pass this on to our Son Alexandre, who you will give birth to carry on the Great Work after we are reunited behind the veil for all eternity.
Love,
Roland
P.S. Boom Boom Boom

I then smiled with eyes full of tears.
When I looked up the attorney had gone outside. I walked to

the front of the chapel to greet the guests, and Bonhommes. My eye caught the attorney as he watched a car pull up the driveway, coming to a stop at the front of the church. Two women casually dressed exited the car, and walked up to the attorney, they both spoke in unison.

"So, do you have our checks?"

The attorney handed them each an envelope, then the two women opened them to review the contents.

"The checks are certified; this should make a comfortable life for both of you. Are you planning to attend the service?"

They responded, "What for – we got the money, are we getting any real estate as well?"

"Have a nice day, ladies, your father extends his love and peace to you."

"Why couldn't he have given us more when he was alive?"

They got back into the car and sped off.

The Bishop gave his final blessing, then handed out signed copies of Roland's book of poems and meditations to all in attendance, asking them to pick out one of their favorites and to read at the reception after the service. The memorial service was purposely held later in the day around sunset.

We then walked over to the tent for the catered reception that included Roland's former band Cygnus Allor, now playing Roland's favorite piece of music, *Falsedatz et desmezura*. After sunset we all gathered in a circle to take a turn reading one of Roland's poems or meditations. Next we walked over to the fire pit, which had a tarp in the center covering a rather large mass. The Bishop directed the guests to listen as he prepared the bonfire. He removed the tarp, which revealed a rather large volume of secular books. The bishop then took one of the urns and sprinkled Roland's ashes over the books, and ignited a flame that soon consumed the books. We then watched and mediated, and prayed for Roland's soul for a peaceful journey up the river to take him home. As the fire was reduced to ashes, the Bishop offered everyone a glass of Absinthe for a final toast to Roland, then poured what was left in our glasses, to be cast into the fire. The bishop then took a mixture of the book ashes and Roland's ashes, combined them in the urn, then walked with me to cast them in the river. We then offered up one final prayer to Roland.

A number of limousines arrived to take many of us to our chartered plane to France. Beth, the Bishop, and the Grand Master of the Illuminati and I were in the lead car, along with Roland's attorney from the U.S., and his attorney from France. We were then informed of how we were to carry on the Great Work for a humanity in distress. We now follow Roland on our arduous path as we have agreed to do. Now with just a few breaths of life in me, I smile with joy, as I recall the first day I entered Roland's class. I do remember the first words he had spoken to the class.

"Today, students, I will take you to a new path and level of learning, a journey that begins in the soul, not for the faint hearted, only for the true seeker of knowledge; many are called though few are chosen."

He spoke to my heart and soul. And, as he turned to me with that Cheshire smile on his face, I then knew my destiny. Now that I have been blessed with the Haggai Sophie that fell upon Beth and I the night before the wedding, it all made sense now. My abusive marriage was not a curse, but a blessing. Now knowing that as one walks through hell, they are guided by heaven's graces. I would never have found this life, had it not been for my bad choice for a first husband.

Roland had the builder carve out a niche in the center of the polished ashlar cornerstone to place one of the urns holding his ashes, for his new Library built in the center of the school atop

Mountsegur. Roland had personally funded this new international School of Gnostic Studies, as directed by the hierarchies according to their specifications, to educate and graduate spiritual leaders and Adepts to guide humanity through the coming upheavals and holocausts that would soon consume the planet.

Roland, along with the bishops, Bonhommes, Grand Masters, mystics, and spiritual Adepts, developed a twelve-year program dedicated to the science of the soul, meditations, study of religions, esoteric languages, rituals, diets, occult knowledge, health, and academic study of philosophy, religion, psychology and psychic development. This intensive program renders a PhD to those who complete its rigorous course of study. Today, the school is recognized as the premier world University of Study. Since its inception, The University of the Bonhommes has turned out a succession of world leaders who now manage the planet with divine stewardship. I have been blessed to play a major role in the building of this spiritual organization, never regretting my decision to give up the profane life, and to live a celibate/spiritual life, cloistered among our spiritual teachers and Bonhommes. Now on the last day of my life, my soul is rich and full of the Divine Light passed on to me. I look forward to being reunited with Roland behind the veil, and Beth who assisted me in this Great Work.

We have proved to the world we are not the heretics as accused by the profane in the past, but the beacon of light that serves humanity under God's guidance. And, the true messengers of God. The world leaders came to us for advice and assistance in the aftermath of the American Civil War of 2020, as the nation tore itself apart. This once-great nation was behaving as a child in puberty too young to govern itself and the world. Americans' shallowness and selfishness ignited a terrible civil war that its enemies were soon to exploit. America blinded itself to the world around it, and fell deaf to our warnings of its coming fate. Americans failed to heed our warnings, as they chose to listen to the demons that promised them prosperity and riches if they would forsake our warnings.

Now drunk with a fool's wisdom, America continued on with its civil war. Now divided, the two opposing sides clashed in the streets, each side backed with divided components of a disorganized military with shaky and changing allegiance. Soon America was nuked first by North Korea, then China, leveling major cities and killing millions in its wake. America now was forced to make internal peace, and the military took over in a brokered coup to restore a unity of command. America consolidated and reorganized by responding with its arsenal of nuclear warheads that reduced North Korea to ashes as it was being attacked by South Korea. China's major cities were devastated.

The nuclear conflagration set off a series of equally damaging tornados, floods, earthquakes and tidal waves, forcing all the nations to recall their troops home from foreign ports. During this madness, Russia was hedging and fearful that America would never be able to lead itself to victory, changed sides only to be nuked by China and America. The Mideast exploded, as all countries launched their nuclear arsenals on targets not knowing if they were allies, enemies or neutral. With all the nations crippled hostilities stopped. The world leaders now approached us to petition the heavens for guidance and to atone for their sins.

With tears of self-pity, and a new-found humility, they prayed to the heavens, unaware their clasped hands were still chained to Satan's greedy and nefarious heart. They lacked the wisdom to understand why God had abandoned them, and would not intercede. Our mystics admonished them, reminding them they had abandoned God for power, greed, hatred and warmongering. And, God had interceded by not acting, letting man destroy himself. Our Great work brokered all the truces and peace agreements, brought all the religions together, by revealing the truths of their faiths, and their errors of their faith created by its leader to build selfish constructs intended to trump God's intentions. We set up a tribunal to judge and sentence all the world leaders for their heinous crimes against humanity. The school set up economic systems that allowed for an even distribution of wealth.

Our Utopian mission is nearing completion, as the world has now learned to live in harmony with itself, nature and the Godhead. Now this Great Work will be turned over to Alexandre to be succeeded by his daughter Sophia, as they make ready the way for the return of the Messiah, to reclaim the devil's earth for the Godhead.

As I began to slip in and out of consciousness, Alexandre and Sophia entered the room, along with the Bishop, to perform my Consolamentum. I passed on Roland's books to Alexandre, along with the third urn containing Roland's ashes. I took off my rosy cross and placed in around his neck. I told him his father's blood, sweat, and tears were contained within it. As the Bishop was performing the Consolamentum, I pulled out a sealed envelope from Roland with my name on it. I unsealed it and read it, silently, to myself:

My Beloved Candice,
Your work is now complete, and we will soon be reunited behind the veil as we enter Heaven's Holy Lodge. Together we will guide Alexandre and Sophia to complete the Great Work, and assist them to make ready for the return of the Messiah. For our arduous paths

were not in vain, for the heavens now bless us for our service to God and His humanity in distress. Now feel autumn's sweet breeze as it caresses your soul, to take you home. Close your eyes in peace and see the beacon of light that shines from Montsegur to the world now mature enough to understand and accept our gift of fraternity for all.

I look forward to your warm embraces and kisses, and the love we will now share for all eternity. Candice, now feel my hand on your heart, and listen to my final song for your mortal ears, to guide you into my awaiting arms.

With Love,

Roland

P.S. Boom Boom Boom

BIBLIOGRAPHY

Alexandrian, Sarane. The Great Work of the Flesh. Rochester, Vermont: Destiny Books, 2000.

Birks, Walter. The Treasure of Montsegur. UK: British Cataloguing in Publication Data, 1987.

Guirdham, Arthur. The Cathars and Reincarnation. USA: Theosophical Publishing House, 1970.

King, Francis. Techniques of High Magic. Rochester, Vermont: Destiny Books, 1976.

Martin, Sean. The Cathars. New York: Shelter Harbor Press, 2016.

McGlynn, Sean. Kill Them All. UK: The History Press, 2015.

Oldenbourg, Zoe. Massacre at Montsegur. New York: George Weidenfeld & Nicolson Ltd., 1961.

O'Shea, Stephen. The Perfect Heresy. UK: Profile Books Ltd., 2000.

Randolph, Paschal Beverly. Magia Sexulis. Rochester, Vermont: Destiny Books, 2012.

Smith, Andrew Philip. The Lost Teachings of the Cathars, UK and USA: Watkins Media Limited, 2015.

Versluis, Arthur. The Secrets of Western Sexual Mysticism. Rochester, Vermont: Destiny Books, 2008.

Wakefield, Walter L. Heresies of the High Middle Ages. New York: Columbia University Press, 1969.

Weis, Rene. The Yellow Cross. New York: Vintage Books, 2002.